mary-kate olsen   ashley olsen

so little time

Check out these other great
so little time
titles:

mary-kate olsen   **ashley** olsen

so little time

the makeover experiment

By Jacqueline Carroll

Based on the series created by Eric Cohen
and Tonya Hurley

▰HarperEntertainment
An Imprint of HarperCollins*Publishers*

A PARACHUTE PRESS BOOK

A PARACHUTE PRESS BOOK

Parachute Publishing, L.L.C.
156 Fifth Avenue, Suite 302
New York, NY 10010

Published by
HarperEntertainment
An *Imprint of* HarperCollins*Publishers*
10 East 53rd Street, New York, NY 10022-5299

Visit HarperEntertainment on the World Wide Web at
www.harpercollins.com

10 9 8 7 6 5 4 3 2 1

chapter
one

"**S**ierra, guess what day this is!" Fourteen-year-old Riley Carlson practically bounced as she followed her best friend, Sierra Pomeroy, into one of the girls' bathrooms at West Malibu High.

"Hmm . . ." Sierra pretended to think. "It's Wednesday, so could it be . . ."

"Yes!" Riley cried. "Today's the day the people from *Total Makeover* are coming!"

Total Makeover was one of Riley's favorite television shows. Last week they had announced a special contest called *Total Teen Makeover*. They were going to four different high schools and would pick one couple from each to be on the show. Riley nearly passed out from excitement when she found out that West Malibu had been selected as one of the high schools.

Riley loved watching the show every night. In each episode the guys were made over according to their girlfriends' directions—clothes, hair, the works. But the makeover wasn't only about a new look. It was about a new lifestyle. So the couples went on dates to places that fit the guy's new image, the cameras catching every moment.

For the teen version a TV crew would follow each couple around for a week, and they'd air clips on the show every night. At the end of the week the television audience would vote for the couple they liked best as the contest winners.

"I hope we get picked!" Riley exclaimed. "It would rock to be on the show!" West Malibu was the last high school the makeover people were visiting, and they would announce their choices tomorrow.

"I know," Sierra said, taking a stretchy purple top from her backpack. Her parents' idea of fashion was seriously last century, so Sierra solved the problem by changing into "cool" clothes before classes started. "It's hard to believe that Charlie agreed to do it with you."

Riley frowned. "Well, actually . . . I haven't asked him yet," she admitted.

"What?" Sierra pulled the top over her head and fluffed out her long red hair. "You haven't asked your boyfriend? This is the only day the makeover people will be here to talk to couples. What are you waiting for?"

"The last minute," Riley said. "If Charlie had time to think about it, he might say no."

"Oh, right. Good point," Sierra agreed.

[Riley: Okay, so I'm a teensy bit worried about getting Charlie to sign up with me for *Total Teen Makeover*. For one thing, Charlie Slater likes himself the way he is, which is total punk: music, clothes, attitude, everything! For another, he refuses to even watch a makeover show with me. He says they're a total waste of time, not to mention brain cells!]

"You have to get Charlie to agree to be on that show," Sierra said, carefully folding her "proper" blue blouse into her backpack. "Can you picture it?" Her eyes widened. "I mean, Charlie's cute, but with a makeover he could be a real hottie."

"*Could* be?" Riley laughed. Sierra was practically as excited as *she* was. "I think he already *is*."

"You know what I mean," Sierra scolded with a grin. "Admit it. Wouldn't you love to see him in something besides a black concert T-shirt?"

Riley grinned back. "Okay, I confess. I've always wondered what Charlie would look like wearing—oh, I don't know—blue. Red. Brown. Anything but black."

She and Sierra giggled at their reflections in the mirror.

Not that I want to change Charlie forever, Riley thought, reapplying her lip gloss. Just for a week. Just long enough to be on the show and maybe even win the contest.

"So, do you have a plan?" Sierra asked, checking her

hair again. "You don't have that much time left."

"Yup," Riley declared. "I'm going to ask him right after *The Morning Rant*."

The Morning Rant was the school radio show she and Charlie did together every day before classes.

"How are you going to talk him into it?" Sierra asked.

"Well, I thought about begging."

Sierra gave her a skeptical look. "Riley Carlson, begging? I don't think so."

"You're right, it would be way too humiliating." Riley took a brush from her backpack and quickly pulled it through her straight, shoulder-length blond hair. "Plus it probably wouldn't work."

"True. So what are you going to do, bribe him?" Sierra asked.

"Hmm . . . I guess you could call it that," Riley admitted. She tossed her hairbrush back into her bag, then smiled broadly at Sierra. "But I have another word for it—*motivation!*"

Chloe Carlson, Riley's twin sister, had a million things on her mind as she hurried toward her locker. Speeding around a corner with her head down, she bumped into someone coming from the opposite direction.

"Oof! Sorry," she said, staggering back.

"Me, too," the guy said. "Hey! Don't I know you?"

"Lennon?" Chloe shook her wavy blond hair out of her eyes so she could see. Sure enough, she'd crashed into Lennon Porter, who just happened to be her boyfriend. Her forehead crinkled as she looked up at him. "What do you mean, 'Don't I know you?'"

"Just kidding," Lennon told her. He shoved his hands into his pockets and shrugged. "Well, sort of. You're kind of hard to find these days."

"Am I?"

"Yeah, so I was hoping we'd run into each other. And we did—ha-ha."

Chloe smiled. Lennon was so sweet and so cute, with his dark curly hair and gray-blue eyes. "I'm really glad to see you!"

"Me, too," Lennon said, giving her a quick kiss. "You're never around."

"I know. I've been so busy," Chloe said. She'd spent the entire weekend helping organize and throw a Sweet Sixteen party for her cousin, Gemma, so she didn't see Lennon at all. They usually ate lunch together on Monday, but Chloe's science class went on an all-day field trip. And she had to cancel last night's pizza date to study for today's English test.

[**Chloe**: Yikes, it's been four whole days! No wonder I'm so happy to see him!]

Chloe thought a second. "This is Wednesday, right?"

"Wow," Lennon said. "You *are* busy if you can't keep track of what day it is."

Chloe gave him a playful smack on the arm.

"*Anyway*," she said, ignoring his teasing, "we have the same lunch period today, so let's eat together."

"Definitely."

"Oh, wait—I can't!" Chloe said, suddenly remembering. "I'm studying for the English test with some of the kids from my class at lunch. I *really* need to be there."

"Well, can we at least hang together after school?"

"Umm . . ." Chloe paused. She was almost positive she had something to do after school. But what?

"Chloe, there you are!" Tara Jordan called out, coming around the corner. She was with Quinn Reyes, one of Chloe's other best friends. "Geez, you're hard to find!"

"That's exactly what I just told her," Lennon said.

"It's not as if I'm hiding, you guys," Chloe told them. "I've just had tons of stuff to do."

"What else is new?" Tara teased, her brown eyes sparkling. "You're like a walking to-do list."

"Just don't forget the dance committee meeting," Quinn reminded Chloe, tucking a strand of curly dark hair behind one ear.

That's it! Chloe thought. That's what I was trying to remember.

"Right after school today," Tara added. "Room one-twelve. Be there or beware!"

"I *knew* I had something to do!" Chloe turned to Lennon as Quinn and Tara walked off. "I'm on the committee for the all-freshmen dance. I absolutely have to be at the first meeting."

Lennon sighed.

"I'm sorry," Chloe said. "I didn't think today would be crazy, but it is. Maybe after the meeting? Oh, wait—no. Mom's showing a new line of clothes next Saturday, and I'm one of the models, so I need to try on some outfits when I get home."

"Oooo-kay," Lennon said.

"Omigosh!" Chloe exclaimed. "Home! That reminds me—did I tell you that a pipe in Riley's and my bathroom sprang a leak?"

Lennon shook his head.

"Major mess!" Chloe said. "It was in one of the walls, so the paint's ruined. I said I'd plan a whole room redo—Riley doesn't care what color, as long as it's not pink—and I need to check out paint and wallpaper samples. And I'm *way* behind in my studying! There's a science test next week and a social studies paper, which I haven't even started yet. . . ." She paused, taking a deep breath. "Whoa! I am so stressed!"

"No kidding," Lennon agreed. "You're talking a mile a minute." He put his hands on her shoulders. "Chloe, you need to chill."

"*Chill*? Remind me what that is again?" Chloe said with a laugh.

Lennon rolled his eyes. "It's also called *relaxing*. Listen, it's great to be busy, but don't you think you're going a little nuts with all the stuff you do? You said it yourself—you're totally stressed."

"I guess. . . ." Chloe said. She *was* feeling a bit like an overstretched rubber band.

"Plus you hardly have time for *me* lately," he added. He ran his hands through his hair, looking a little exasperated. "It's like I need an appointment to see you."

[**Chloe**: Okay, that's definitely an exaggeration. But still, when was the last time Lennon and I spent any real time together? When was the last time I wasn't in the middle of some humongous project or trying to remember the gazillion things I have to do? I know. You don't have a clue. Guess what? Neither do I!]

"I'm sorry, Lennon," Chloe said. "I can't believe I've been ignoring one of the most important people in my life—you!"

Lennon blushed a little. "Well, I didn't mean to complain."

"Oh, yes, you did," Chloe teased. "But that's okay. You're right. I want to be with you, too. I definitely need some chill time, and I'm going to take it—I promise!"

"Great," Lennon said. "We'll talk later."

"Later." Chloe gave him a quick kiss and hurried away.

Relax and spend time with Lennon, Chloe thought. She put it at the very top of her mental to-do list. But with everything else she had to do, she couldn't help wondering how she'd keep her promise.

• • •

"That was Bittersweet's latest release, 'Breakaway,'" Riley said into the studio microphone. "I played it, so you know I liked it. What about you, Charlie?"

"Not bad," Charlie admitted.

Riley gasped dramatically. "Did you hear that, everybody? Charlie Slater, King of Punk, Emperor of Alternative, actually admitted to liking Bittersweet!"

"I didn't say that," Charlie said. "I said it wasn't *bad*. Which isn't the same thing as *good*. *Here's* good." He cued a song from a Sledge CD, punched the button, and leaned back in his chair, grinning at Riley.

Riley grinned back. She loved doing *The Morning Rant*. Sitting in West Malibu High's small radio studio with Charlie was a great way to start the day, even if she didn't like his musical choices.

Doing the show was how they met, and from the beginning they'd argued about what music to play. He wanted alternative and punk. Riley liked almost everything *but* alternative and punk. They finally compromised, with each getting time for their favorite music. But that didn't stop the arguing, even on the air.

[Riley: The kids at school loved it, which was a major surprise. An even bigger surprise was that we discovered we love each other!]

Charlie pushed the MUTE button on his and Riley's microphones. "Guess what," he said. "You know that radio station, K-SUN?"

"ALL-*ternative*, ALL *the time*?" Riley said. "Sure. I hear it every time I scan the dial. Then I skip over it really fast," she added, just to get a reaction.

"Too complex for you, huh?" Charlie shot back.

"Oh, yeah. I'm just a simple surfer girl." Riley laughed. "Okay, what about K-SUN?"

Charlie smiled. "You might not be skipping over it so fast in the future. Not if you want to catch their newest DJ."

"Newest DJ? Who . . . ?" She paused, noticing the excited look in Charlie's brown eyes. "You mean *you*? Really?"

Charlie nodded. "They need a part-time DJ on the weekends. I had an interview yesterday with the manager."

Riley's eyes widened. "And he hired you on the spot!" she exclaimed.

Charlie laughed. "Not quite. He said there were two other people up for the job, and he wants to listen to the shows we're doing now before he decides. But he told me I have a really good chance."

"Charlie, that is so great!" Riley leaned over and gave him a kiss. "You're going to get it—I'm positive! Nobody could be better than you. And I promise to tune in every second you're on the air."

Charlie raised an eyebrow.

"Okay, I might turn the music down—way down," Riley admitted. "But I'll definitely listen to *you*."

Charlie squeezed her hand, then turned their microphones back on as the Sledge song ended. "Okay, folks, that was seriously good, wasn't it? Riley's turn now, for the final cut of the morning. I hope it isn't so lame that it ruins your day."

"Ha-ha," Riley said. "I hope it repairs the ear damage done by Charlie's last pick."

She cued up a song from Wazzup?, then turned back to Charlie. Okay, it's now or never, she thought.

Crossing her fingers, she told him about the *Total Teen Makeover* contest.

"Oh, no, no way!" Charlie declared, shaking his head. "A makeover show? Get real. The people on them are major sellouts. It's so uncool."

"No, it's not. It's fun!" Riley argued. "And most people look way better at the end. What's wrong with that?"

Running a hand through his unruly brown hair, Charlie glanced down at his frayed black jeans and Frakture T-shirt. "What's the matter with the way I look?" he asked.

"Hmm . . . where should I start?" Riley deadpanned.

Charlie glanced at her. "You're kidding, right?"

"Of course I'm kidding!" Riley laughed. "If I didn't like the way you look, I would have said something a long time ago."

"True," Charlie agreed. "You definitely say what's on your mind."

"And anyway, you only have to change for the show," Riley reminded him. "It's for a week, not forever."

"Yeah, but . . . ."

"Besides, how can you be so sure you won't have fun?" Riley said. "You've decided that makeover shows are dumb without even watching a single one!"

Charlie grinned. "Are you accusing me of not giving them a chance?"

"Yep. And aren't you the one who always says people should be open to new experiences?" Riley asked.

"Okay, you got me on that," Charlie admitted. He gave her a long look. "You really want to do this, don't you?"

Riley nodded.

He shrugged. "Okay, then. I'm game."

"Thank you, Charlie!" Riley gave him a kiss. "It really means a lot to me."

[Riley: He's doing it to make me happy. Isn't that great? I didn't even have to use my so-called motivation. But wait until he hears the rest—he'll really be glad he said yes.]

"Look, I know you think makeover shows are silly and a total waste of time," Riley said. "But if we win, it'll definitely be worth it."

"Oh, yeah? What's the prize?" Charlie asked. "Seaweed baths and mud on my face? Or maybe a brain transplant?"

"How did you know?" Riley joked. "No, the prizes are a cover photo on *California Teen* magazine . . ."

Charlie rolled his eyes.

"A*nd*," Riley continued, "a choice between an all-expenses-paid night in L.A.—clothes, limo, dinner, movie opening—or a free shopping spree at the L.A. store of our choice."

Charlie straightened up in his chair. "Our choice?" he repeated. "Any L.A. store?"

Riley nodded. "Let's just say we win. Gee, I wonder which store you would pick."

[Riley: As if I didn't know!]

"L.A. Music Factory," Charlie replied instantly. "They have the most amazing inventory."

"You could fill a cart with every CD you ever wanted and not have to pay a penny! Wouldn't that be awesome?" Riley asked.

Charlie nodded. "So what do we do now?"

"First we have to get picked to be on the show," Riley explained.

"Okay," Charlie agreed. "So let's go for it."

Riley gave him another kiss. "Thank you, Charlie! And no matter what happens, we're going to have a blast—just wait and see!"

chapter
two

Chloe looked at the group of kids sitting around Room 112 after classes. She took a deep breath. She wasn't sure how they were going to react to her announcement.

"Thanks for asking me to chair the dance committee, everybody," she said. "But I can't do it."

"What do you mean?" Margot asked. "You head committees all the time."

"Yeah, if you're in charge, everything will get done, for sure," Sam agreed. "You're like, majorly organized."

Chloe was flattered, but she'd promised Lennon to find some chill time. Not heading up the dance committee was a good way to start.

"Thanks," she said again. "But I really can't be in charge of another project right now."

"Okay, so let's have co-chairs," Quinn suggested. "Chloe, me, and Tara. That way you're not totally in charge."

Tara nodded. "I'm in. If it's okay with everybody else," she added.

"That seems okay, I guess," Chloe said.

Everyone quickly agreed, and after discussing the dance's theme, decorations, food, and music, the group broke for the day.

Great, Chloe thought as she left and headed home. Operation Chill has begun. I'm feeling more relaxed already.

"This is gorgeous, Mom," Chloe declared an hour later, pirouetting in the living room of the Carlsons' beach house. She wore a deep-purple silk dress her mother had designed. Very formal and refined. It wasn't Chloe's style, but it *was* beautiful. "Classical Elegance is the perfect name for your new line."

"I like it, too," Macy Carlson said, tapping a note into her Palm Pilot with one hand as she flipped through a pad of paper with the other. "Let's hope the business execs agree."

"How could they not agree?" Manuelo del Valle said from the doorway. "They would have to be *loco!*"

[**Chloe**: Manuelo has been with our family since Riley and I were born. If you asked him what his job is, he'd say he's our full-time cook and house-keeper. If you asked me, I'd say he's our full-time friend.]

"Manuelo is right, Mom," Chloe said. "Once they see your designs, the business people are going to promote your new line to the max."

"Thanks, you two." Macy smiled. "But a slick presentation will help, too. Let's see, I've booked the Garden Room—very elegant, with all that sculpture and marble. And I hired Catering to Malibu for the food, so that's all set."

"Ooh, yum!" Chloe said. "They make the best shrimp puffs on the planet."

Manuelo cleared his throat. "The *planet*?"

"Except for yours, of course." Chloe laughed.

"Let's see," Macy said, frowning at her list. "The printer promised the programs by next Thursday, but I'll check with them tomorrow, just in case."

Chloe nodded. Her mom seemed to have everything pretty much under control. "What music are you going to use?"

Macy shook her head. "I guess I'll burn a CD, but I'm not sure what to put on it. Hip-hop or rock wouldn't really go with such formal clothes."

"Hey, what about live music?" Chloe suggested. "Like a little instrumental group. They could play all kinds of music, including classical. Classical Elegance, get it?"

"That's perfect, Chloe!" Macy declared, tapping more notes into her Palm Pilot.

"Ooh, and if there are any women in the group, they could wear your designs!" Chloe added.

Macy nodded eagerly and made another note.

Manuelo chuckled and shook his head.

"What?" Chloe asked. "Don't you think it's a good idea, Manuelo?"

"It's a brilliant idea, my little scone," he said. "No, I was just thinking how much like your mother you are becoming."

"Me? Like Mom?" Chloe asked.

"You don't see it?" Manuelo said as he smiled. "You are both always coming up with ideas and plans, how to do this and how to manage that. Always busy like the beetles."

"Bees," Macy murmured without glancing up.

"Those, too," Manuelo agreed.

"Just bees," Macy said, switching to the notepad. "*Bee*, actually. *Busy as a bee.*"

[Chloe: Bees, beetles—who cares? Manuelo is right—I'm turning into my mother! Not that I don't love and admire her, you understand. But nobody wants to be exactly like her mother. Especially when I just promised my boyfriend I'd relax and spend more time with him!]

Manuelo shook his head. "I don't know how you both do so many things at once."

My brain just leaps into overdrive, Chloe thought. Here I am, ready to start giving Mom advice on her project, when I still have tons to do myself. In fact, she realized, I didn't really give up the dance committee—I just spread the stress around a bit.

[Chloe: I've got to stop this—now!]

"Mom, I need to call somebody," Chloe said. "Is it okay if I change?"

"What?" Macy glanced up. "Oh, sure, honey, go ahead."

Chloe hurried upstairs and changed out of the Classical Elegance dress into Capris and a butter-yellow T-shirt. Classical comfort, she thought as she punched in Tara's cell-phone number.

"Can you and Quinn co-chair the dance committee without me?" Chloe asked after Tara answered.

"I guess so, but why?" Tara asked.

"Because I've been doing too much," Chloe explained. "I'm totally stressed, but I keep getting involved in project after project. It's getting out of control."

"So you're going to quit—just like that?" Tara asked. "Cold turkey?"

"It's the best way," Chloe agreed. "No more organizing things, no more micromanaging, no more being busy as a beetle."

"Bee," Tara said.

"Whatever. Anyway, I'd be happy to burn some CDs for the dance," Chloe said, "but I really don't want to handle anything else. I need some major downtime. Besides, the committee doesn't need three co-chairs."

"Well, okay," Tara said doubtfully. "Quinn and I can do it. But it's kind of weird to hear you talk about downtime."

"I know," Chloe agreed. "It feels weird to say it. But I'm going to do it. The 'new' Chloe starts right now!"

Chloe hung up, feeling pleased with herself. She headed downstairs for a snack and heard her mother on the phone. Macy was talking in her usual rapid-fire way about finding a string quartet for the fashion presentation.

No, not just strings, Chloe thought. You've got to have drums and a piano, too, or it'll be way too formal.

Chloe veered toward her mother's home office to discuss it. But as she passed the kitchen, she saw Manuelo flipping through paint and wallpaper samples.

Oh, right, the bathroom, Chloe thought. I have to talk to Manuelo about that. She started into the kitchen, then stopped.

What am I doing? she asked herself. The new, de-stressed Chloe would just walk on by, right? Mom is perfectly capable of picking a musical group. And Manuelo has great taste. I'm supposed to relax and let things happen.

Wow, Chloe thought. Relaxing is harder than I thought.

Then she smiled. She knew the perfect relaxation consultant.

Chloe left the house and soon arrived at her father's home in a trailer park called Vista del Mar.

"Dad?" Chloe called.

Jake Carlson stuck his head around the end of the small trailer on the bluff overlooking the beach. "I'm on the deck, honey!" he hollered, pushing his horn-rimmed glasses up on his nose. "Come join me for the show!"

[Chloe: Dad means the sunset. He tries to watch it almost every night. He says it keeps him "one with the universe." See, Dad used to run the fashion design business with Mom. But then he decided he wanted to find himself. They split up (they're still good friends), Mom took over the business, and Dad found himself . . . in yoga, meditation, and a trailer on the beach.]

"Whoa, it's gorgeous!" Chloe commented, gazing at the red and pink clouds as she climbed up to the tiny deck.

"I call it my nature channel," Jake said, sighing peacefully.

Chloe gave her father a kiss. "Dad, I need your help."

"Sure, honey. What is it?"

"I need to learn how to relax," she told him. "And I mean *really* relax, like you do."

Jake's eyes lit up. "Great! Everybody should. I can give you a book or two, but right now let's just drink in the sunset. Sit down here with me."

Chloe sat cross-legged on the deck next to her father.

"Take nice, slow breaths. Like this." Jake breathed in deeply, then said "Ohm" when he exhaled.

Chloe stared at him.

"Try it," he urged.

Chloe shut her eyes and took in a deep breath. She let out a slow exhale and made a little "ohm" sound.

[Chloe: Honestly? I feel very weird saying "ohm." But I'm going to keep trying it. After all, look at Dad—he went from uptight to laid-back in record time. If anybody can show me how to de-stress, it's Dad.]

Jake grinned. "I think you've got it."

"All right, West Malibu High couples, this is the moment!" Dash Gilford, the young, hip host of *Total Makeover*, declared. "Is everybody ready?"

It was Thursday afternoon after school. Riley and Charlie were sitting with a bunch of other couples in the auditorium, waiting to hear who had been chosen to be on *Total Teen Makeover*.

"Before I announce the lucky couple, I want to thank everybody for signing up and going through the interview yesterday," Dash continued. "You're just terrific. If I had my way, every one of you would appear on our special teen show!"

"I bet he says that to all the couples," Charlie whispered to Riley.

"Shh!" Riley scolded Charlie. Okay, Dash Gilford was definitely always "on." And with his perfectly highlighted blond hair and his fashion-magazine clothes, he was exactly the kind of "mainstream" guy Charlie was always putting down.

But Riley didn't mind Dash—or his style. Plus he seemed genuinely nice. Yesterday afternoon, when he interviewed her and Charlie, he joked around a lot. He even laughed when Charlie admitted that the main reason he wanted to be on the show was the chance for a free shopping trip at L.A. Music Factory.

[Riley: I could have died, but Dash actually thanked Charlie for being honest!]

"To show our appreciation," Dash went on, "we'd like to give each couple a little gift—an official *Total Makeover* T-shirt!"

Riley bit her lip as she watched Miri, Dash's assistant, pass out bright blue shirts with the show's logo on the front. A T-shirt was nice, but Riley wanted to know who'd been picked!

Will they just hurry up and make the announcement already? she thought. This waiting is driving me crazy!

She checked out some of the guys. Kevin was cute, but there was definitely room for improvement. And what about Eddie, the joker in her history class? He'd have a blast getting made over. If Riley didn't want to be on the show so badly, she'd root for him because he'd be so much fun to watch.

"All right, if everyone has a T-shirt . . ." Dash said as he scanned the room.

Riley raised her hand. "Sorry, but you missed Charlie and me," she said.

"Riley Carlson and Charlie Slater? Miri, don't you have T-shirts for them?" Dash asked.

Miri shook her head, her straight black bangs brushing her dark eyebrows.

"Well, gee, you two, I'm sorry," Dash said with a frown. "I guess you didn't get them because . . ." Suddenly his frown disappeared, replaced by a television host's megawatt smile. ". . . because you'll be getting yours *after* you've appeared on *Total Teen Makeover!*"

"Oh, wow!" Riley gasped. "Really?"

"Absolutely!" Dash grinned.

Riley gave Charlie a hug. "I can't believe it!"

"Me neither," Charlie said. He was smiling, but Riley could tell he was less than thrilled. "Seriously, I can't believe I'm going to do this."

"Believe it, Charlie." Dash laughed. "Tomorrow at the mall, you'll begin your transformation from punk to California Cool, as Riley asked for on your application."

Charlie rolled his eyes.

[Riley: Charlie may be skeptical now, but once we get started he'll have fun. He'll see what a great idea this is!]

chapter
three

"Oh, man, Pacific Male?" Charlie groaned, staring at the men's clothing store.

It was the next day after school, and Charlie, Riley, and the *Total Makeover* crew were at the mall—the first stop on the transformation trail. As usual, Charlie wore black jeans, black combat boots, and a black T-shirt with the logo of a band Riley had never heard of.

Charlie grinned at Riley. "Could it be any more mainstream?"

Riley laughed. "Well, there's always Gentlemanly Attire," she teased. "Lots of tweed and leather elbow patches."

"Tempting . . . but no," Charlie said. He peered into the display window of Pacific Male.

"See anything you like, Charlie?" Dash asked.

Dash and Miri stood on either side of Dave, the cameraman, a young, bald guy with a thick red beard.

With them were two more members of the crew, a curly-haired woman named Shelby, who held a boom mike, and Todd, a thin man in charge of lighting. All of them wore *Total Makeover* T-shirts.

"Those pants aren't bad," Charlie said, gesturing to one of the mannequins.

Riley rolled her eyes. "They're black," she pointed out.

Charlie grinned. "Yeah, but they're not jeans. Doesn't that count?"

Riley slipped her arm into Charlie's and laughed. "Don't be afraid. I won't let the clothes hurt you."

She was having a great time. They'd drawn a small crowd the minute they arrived at the mall, and it kept getting bigger. Glancing over her shoulder, Riley spotted Sierra with a group of kids. Sierra grinned and gave her a thumbs-up.

Riley waved, then turned back to Charlie. "Come on, let's go in," she said. "And don't worry, you won't have to try on any three-piece suits or ties."

"Is that a promise?" Charlie joked.

"Promise," Riley said.

Charlie nodded and straightened up. "Okay, I'm ready to turn into Mr. California Cool."

"All right!" Dash cried. "Let's go shopping!"

Riley took Charlie's hand and walked with him past the camera into the store. Trailed by the crew, the two of them began checking out the clothes.

[Riley: Actually, I checked out the clothes. Charlie just stood in the center of the store in a daze. He was being a good sport, but I think he was in major denial!]

"Okay, I'm coming out," Charlie called from the dressing room forty minutes later. "I don't suppose you can turn the camera off."

"Ha!" Dash chortled. "Fat chance!"

"I didn't think so," Charlie said. "Okay, are you ready?"

Wearing dark tan khakis and a soft deep-red shirt, Charlie stepped out of the dressing room.

[Riley: Wow!]

"Wow!" Miri echoed Riley's thought. "You clean up nice, Charlie!"

"Great choices, Riley!" Dash exclaimed. He rushed to Charlie's side, followed by Shelby holding the boom mike over their heads. "Charlie, what do you think?"

Before Charlie could answer, the salesman poked his head into camera range. "Very nice," he commented. He glanced at Charlie's black combat boots. "But the shoes absolutely have to go."

Riley nodded. The boots did *not* fit with Charlie's new look. "Right. Let's see some tennis shoes."

"I have tennis shoes," Charlie protested.

"I mean ones that aren't falling apart," Riley teased.

"Those are the best kind," Charlie declared. "It took

a whole year to break them in. My feet won't know what hit them."

"Your feet will thank you," Riley shot back.

Half an hour, three pairs of shoes, and six full shopping bags later, the entourage swept into Hair by Max, a trendy salon. Max himself, a handsome man with flashing white teeth, sat Charlie in front of a huge mirror. He gazed critically at Charlie's long, uncontrollable brown hair.

"What shampoo do you use? Something containing chlorine, perhaps?" Max asked.

"Hey, how'd you guess?" Charlie asked.

Max looked appalled.

"He's joking," Riley said.

"Ah. Well, your hair is dry, but daily use of a conditioning rinse will take care of that," Max said. "Now, as to the style, you've agreed to getting it cut, correct? And your parents approve?"

Charlie laughed. "Are you kidding? My parents can't wait. This is like a birthday present to them."

Max smiled. "Good. So I'm thinking longer in front than in back, and we'll let it fall naturally onto your forehead. And as a final touch, some temporary highlights."

"You mean, like, purple or something?" Charlie asked hopefully.

"What about it, Riley?" Dash asked. "It's your call, remember!"

Riley shook her head. "Purple's too punk for your new look," she told Charlie.

"Oh, yeah," Charlie said. "I keep forgetting. Okay, so what color highlights go with California Cool? Whatever *that* is."

"Your hair will just be lighter brown in places," Riley explained. "As if you're in the sun a lot."

"Exactly," Max agreed.

"I *am* in the sun a lot," Charlie argued.

"I know, but your hair doesn't get lighter," Riley pointed out. "It'll look great. You'll see!"

Max's assistant whisked Charlie away for a shampoo and five minutes later whisked him back to the chair. While Dave filmed, Max went to work trimming Charlie's hair and then painting the highlights into it. Then, after a session with the blow-dryer, Max spun the chair around so Riley and the crew could get the full effect.

[Riley: Double-wow!]

"Lookin' good, Charlie!" Dash declared. "Definitely California Cool!"

"Oooh, yeah!" a voice called out sarcastically. "Want us to start calling you *Charles*?"

Riley whirled around and spotted Jesse and Frodo, two of Charlie's scruffiest punk friends, standing with a small crowd gathered at the front of the salon. She had recognized Jesse's voice. He was tall, with a dragon tattoo running up his neck all the way onto his face. Brown-haired Frodo was much shorter, with six piercings in each ear and a taunting grin.

Charlie grinned back at them. "You can call me Charles, but only if I can call you idiots!"

"No, I have a better name for you," Frodo chuckled, putting on a terrible British accent. "Chas!"

"Ah! Chas, of course!" Jesse agreed, imitating the accent. "Where are you off to next, Chas? A round of golf?"

"Absolutely," Charlie shot back. "And I'd invite you lowlifes, but the golf course has a rule—no dirt bags allowed!" He turned to Riley. "Tell me we're not playing golf," he murmured.

"We're not playing golf." Riley laughed. Charlie was giving as good as he got, but still, she could tell he was uncomfortable with his friends' teasing. "Don't pay any attention to those two. They don't have a clue what they're talking about. You look really cool."

"Right." Charlie nodded and gave a thumbs-up to the camera. "California Cool, that's me."

"Yeah," Riley agreed, grinning at Frodo and Jesse. "Get used to it, guys!"

With a deep sigh Chloe slowly brought her hands palm to palm, completing the Sun Salutation yoga pose. Flickering candles perched on the vanity and the windowsill filled the room with the scent of freesia. The melodic sounds of ocean waves hitting the shore filled the air.

Talk about mellowing out, Chloe thought. This

Sounds of Nature CD Dad gave me really de-stresses. I'm going to do this meditation every single day.

"Chloe, are you still chanting in there?" Riley called from the other side of the door.

"Meditating," Chloe murmured, opening her eyes and coming out of the pose. "Come on in."

Riley stuck her head inside. "Whoa. Smells like an aroma spa in here!"

Chloe nodded. "Isn't it great? It's sooo relaxing."

"Yeah, well, don't get so relaxed you forget to watch our clips on *Total Makeover* tonight," Riley said.

"Are you kidding? My little sister, on television?" Chloe grinned. She enjoyed being the "older sister," even if it was by only eight minutes. "I wouldn't miss it!"

"Good. A bunch of us are going to watch together at the Newsstand," Riley told her. "Want to come?"

Chloe considered. The Newsstand, an Internet café and coffee bar, was a favorite hangout. Tonight it would be crowded and noisy—just the kind of atmosphere Chloe wanted to avoid, at least for a while. Besides, Lennon wasn't going to be there, since the debate team was having a practice tonight. "I think I'll stay here and watch with Mom and Manuelo," she decided.

"Gee, that sounds exciting," Riley joked. "Wait—is this part of the new, low-stress lifestyle you told me about?"

Chloe nodded. "Right. It's not just low-stress, it's a whole new way of looking at what's important. Like, watching you on television is important, but *where* I watch isn't. Being wired twenty-four-seven isn't important either, so I turned off my computer and cell phone."

Riley's eyes widened. "Seriously? I'd go nuts without my cell. Not to mention e-mail."

"I thought I would, too," Chloe said. "Of course, it's only been two days, but I actually haven't missed them. It's amazing!"

Riley looked doubtful, then shrugged. "Well, whatever works for you . . ."

After Riley left, Chloe did another Sun Salutation. Then she blew out each of the candles and went downstairs to make herself some tea. Mug in hand, she joined Macy and Manuelo in the living room to watch *Total Makeover*.

"What are you drinking?" Macy asked, sniffing the air as Chloe sat next to her on the couch.

"It's called Mellow Bliss tea. It's herbal," Chloe explained. "Dad told me about it. He taught me some yoga and meditation techniques too. I've been kind of stressed lately."

"I know the feeling," Macy declared, sipping from her WOMAN AT WORK coffee mug.

"There they are!" Manuelo said, pointing as a video collage of the four couples in the contest came on the TV screen. "Riley is beaming to beat the band! But Charlie . . ." Manuelo shook his head and clucked his tongue.

Chloe giggled. Charlie was smiling, but he definitely looked uptight. He ought to try yoga, she thought.

"Welcome to *Total Makeover!*" Dash Gilford cried, his smile even brighter than Riley's. "Tonight we start our special teen edition, where four lucky high school couples compete for the top prize. Tonight you'll see clips of the guys being transformed from head to toe! As you know, we'll be filming the couples going on dates all week, and you'll see that, too. And next Friday, we'll be taking your votes! For now, sit back and enjoy the segment we call 'Do's and Duds'!"

Sitting cross-legged on the couch, Chloe watched eagerly and kept her fingers crossed for her sister and Charlie. In between quick-cuts and Dash's voice-over narration, the show followed the four couples through boutiques, department stores, and hair salons, catching their discussions about styles and colors and what "look" the girls were going for.

The girl from North Malibu High wanted her boyfriend to "totally lose the baggies" and wear clothes that fit. Pacific View High's boyfriend started out in cutoffs and a too-tight tee and emerged in cargos and a camp shirt. The guy from the private Dunes School had stringy blond hair, a scattering of zits, and a bad slump, not to mention zero taste in clothes. And then there was Charlie.

"He looks so different!" Macy cried when Charlie's transformation was revealed at Hair by Max.

"And so cute!" Chloe added. She really liked Charlie, but she was not a major fan of his personal style.

"But so not happy," Manuelo declared.

"What do you mean? He's smiling," Macy argued.

Manuelo shook his head. "The truth is in the eyes," he intoned.

[Chloe: At that moment Frodo and Jesse decided to act like total fools in front of the camera, so I checked out Charlie's eyes. Maybe Manuelo was right. Charlie's mouth said, *I'm having fun*, but his eyes said, *Help!*]

When the show ended, the crowd at the Newsstand burst into cheers, calling for Riley to take a bow.

Riley stood up from the table where she was sitting with Sierra, Jenna, and Marta. "Thank you, everybody!" she declared. "I'm sure Charlie would thank you, too, but he's working at his dad's shop tonight."

Riley sat back down, her cheeks flushed. "That was *so* cool!" she said. "I still can't believe I'm—I mean *we're*—on a major television show!"

Sierra grinned. "I still can't believe how hot Charlie looked. I mean, wow!"

"That's exactly what I thought," Riley agreed.

"He was cute, for sure," Jenna said, sipping some latte. "So was the guy from the Dunes School. Once they got done with him."

"Yeah, talk about a transformation," Marta said. "Of course, *any* change would have made that guy look better."

"But Charlie looked the best," Sierra declared. "I mean, his hair was fantastic. Loved the highlights! And that dark red shirt was a totally perfect color for him."

"Down, girl," Marta said. "Charlie's not available, remember?"

Sierra rolled her eyes. "Can I help it if his new look just blew me away?"

Riley laughed. Who could blame Sierra for liking California Cool Charlie? This was so much fun. She couldn't wait for the next filming session!

When *Total Makeover* ended, Macy headed for her office to work on her upcoming presentation.

Manuelo turned to Chloe. "Think *faux*," he said.

Chloe blinked. "Huh? Foe? As in enemy? Friend or . . . ?"

"No, no, no, *faux*. For your bathroom," he explained. "A *faux* finish, to fool the eye and make the walls resemble something such as, oh . . . adobe. Or marble would be marvelous!"

"Ooh, that sounds great!" Chloe said. "Or we could paint a *faux* windowsill with plants on it. I can do a kind of blueprint first."

"Yes!" Manuelo agreed.

"No!" Chloe said suddenly. She was doing it again—

leaping head-first into a new project. If she didn't stop herself, she'd be up to her neck in paint samples and books on *faux* painting techniques!

"It's a great idea, Manuelo," Chloe told him. "But I'm really trying to stop taking on project after project. If you pick the paint—anything but pink—I'll help do the work. Is that okay?"

Manuelo nodded. "Of course, my little teabag. I almost forgot you are Zen-ing your way to a new lifestyle."

Laughing, Chloe rinsed out her mug and took Pepper, the family cocker spaniel, for a walk on the beach. At first ideas for the bathroom kept popping into her head, but by the time she got back home, her mind was calm and clear.

Manuelo glanced up from the newspaper spread open on the kitchen table. "Ah, Chloe, Lennon called while you were out. He has been trying to reach you on your cell phone and got worried when you didn't call back. I assured him you were blissfully fine," he added.

"Thanks, Manuelo." Chloe filled the dog's water bowl, then went upstairs, powered up her phone, and punched in Lennon's cell number. "Hi, it's me," she said when he answered. "I'm sorry I didn't call back sooner." She explained about turning off her phone. "And guess what? I'm doing all kinds of stuff to relax—yoga and meditation and everything! I feel totally awesome!"

"Cool. Listen, I was hoping we could get together tonight, but I guess it's too late," Lennon told her.

Chloe heard some strange sounds in the background. "Where are you?" she asked.

"When I couldn't get you, I went over to Marshall's house," Lennon explained. "That's where I am now. A bunch of us are playing pool."

"Oh, that's what I'm hearing," Chloe said, recognizing the thwack of the pool balls. "But why is it too late? It's only eight o'clock."

"I have to leave in a few minutes," Lennon said. "My grandmother's flying in from Chicago, and I'm going with Dad to pick her up."

"Oh. Well, I guess it *is* too late," Chloe said. "But don't worry, we'll be seeing plenty of each other from now on. You told me to chill, and I'm definitely chillin', dude!"

Lennon laughed. "Think you could unchill long enough to have lunch with Grandmother and me?" he asked. "I talk about you so much, she wants to meet you."

"Sure! I'd love to meet her, too," Chloe said.

"Great. When's good for you?"

Chloe automatically turned to her computer, where her weekly planner was always open. But the computer screen was blank. She started to click it on, then stopped. The weekly planner was part of the "old" Chloe, the one who kept running to-do lists in her head and thought *chill* was what a refrigerator did.

"Why don't you and your grandmother pick a day and time?" she said to Lennon. "I'm totally open. Just let me know, and the new Chloe will be there."

chapter
four

"Thanks for calling, Jenna!" Riley said into the phone on Saturday. "Don't forget to vote for us next Friday! Great! Bye."

Riley grinned as she closed her cell phone. "I feel like a celebrity! My phone started ringing at eight this morning, before I was even awake!"

"The price of fame—you've just gotta accept it, Riley," Larry Slotnick said, leaning against a counter. A tall, lanky guy with spiky hair, Larry was in the same class as Riley and Chloe. He was also their next-door neighbor, and he spent as much time in their kitchen as he did in his own.

"Whoa!" Larry paused with one hand on a cupboard door. "I just realized—I'm actually touching *Riley Carlson's* kitchen cabinet! One that *she's* touched!" He gazed at his hand. "I'm never going to wash it again."

Riley laughed and rolled her eyes. Larry was being

goofy, which was nothing new. "Don't worry, Larry, I promise I won't forget you in my climb to the top. You'll still get to come over and rummage for food."

"Well, in that case . . ." Larry pulled open the cupboard and shuffled through some cans and boxes. "What is this, oats?" he asked, pulling out a clear bag of brown, grainy-looking stuff. "Did you get a horse and not tell me?"

"It's millet," Riley told him. "Chloe bought it."

"Chloe got a horse?"

Riley explained Chloe's new laid-back lifestyle. "It includes less sugar and less of everything else that tastes good," she added.

"Millet is delicious!" Chloe's voice called.

"Chloe?" Riley peered through the sliding doors to the deck. Her sister sat in the sun, legs crossed, hands resting, palms up on her thighs. "I thought you went for a walk."

"I did," Chloe replied, moving only her lips. "Now I'm centering myself."

"Cool. Can I watch?" Larry said. Taking the bag of millet with him, he wandered out to the deck.

Riley's phone rang. "Hello?"

"Riley, hi!" Sierra said. "Okay, spill—what's the new and hot Charlie wearing today?"

Riley smiled. Sierra was obviously still blown away by Charlie's transformation. "It's up to him now," she said. "Except he has to wear something we bought yesterday, naturally."

"I hope he wears blue," Sierra decided. "He'd look awesome in blue. Dark green, too. He is *so* cute now, I can't believe it!"

[Riley: **Wow, Sierra's totally gaga! It's weird— she's usually much cooler about things—but I guess I can't blame her. The new Charlie really *is* awesome-looking!]**

"Other than the Dunes School guy, Charlie was the most changed," Sierra went on. "But, like I said, he was definitely the best-looking."

"I think so, too," Riley agreed. "Listen, I've got to go figure out what I'*m* wearing today. I'll talk to you later, okay?"

"Definitely. Tell Charlie hi from me," Sierra said. "Tell him I said to wear blue!"

"Another fan?" Larry called from the deck as Riley hung up.

"You could say that," Riley replied. "It was Sierra. She totally loves Charlie's new look."

"He *did* look cute," Chloe agreed as she moved into another yoga pose. "Kind of uncomfortable, though."

"You mean because of Jesse and Frodo?" Riley asked. "Were they juvenile or what? But Charlie handled them."

"Yeah, but it wasn't just Jesse and Frodo," Chloe said. "I mean, Charlie joked and smiled and all, but I could tell he was uptight underneath."

Riley frowned. She couldn't have missed that, could she? "Really?"

Chloe nodded. "I could give you some relaxation exercises to show him."

Charlie Slater doing yoga? Riley couldn't see it. His idea of kicking back was to hop onto his skateboard or have a listening marathon with every Sledge CD ever recorded.

Riley thanked her sister for the offer, then went upstairs and changed into her favorite denim skirt and a turquoise tank top. She brushed her hair, slipped on the turquoise bracelet Charlie gave her when they first got together, and ran back downstairs. She was totally pumped and couldn't wait to film the next segment.

Who wants to relax, anyway? she thought as she saw the *Total Makeover* van pulling in down the street. Feeling the excitement is a major part of the fun!

"Hey, look, it's *Chas*!" a mocking voice called from the crowd of onlookers outside the cineplex.

Riley rolled her eyes. She knew without even looking that it was Jesse. Which meant Frodo would be next.

"Yeah. In more new threads! Where's your tie, *Chas*?" Frodo hollered.

The two buddies practically fell over laughing. Riley felt a strong urge to stick her tongue out at them.

[Riley: Luckily I remembered I was on camera and kept smiling! Anyway, what those doofusses

know about style wouldn't fill a Post-It note. Charlie looks totally California Cool: cargo pants and a French-blue shirt, with the shirttail out and sleeves rolled up.]

Dash Gilford laughed, flashing his bright white teeth. "Well, Charlie, it looks like your two friends are back. And I don't think they've changed their opinion of your transformation!"

Riley glanced at Charlie. He was smiling, but she could tell he didn't mean it. Maybe Chloe was right, and he *was* a little uptight. Was his jaw actually clenched?

"Anything you want to say to them, Charlie?" Dash asked.

"Yeah, Chas, go ahead," Frodo called. "You can be honest."

"Okay." Charlie kept his fake smile on. "How about, take a hike?"

Exactly what Riley felt like saying. Except they were on television, and she really didn't want the guys to get into a serious insult match.

"Come on, let's get our tickets!" she said to Charlie. Grabbing Charlie's hand, she dragged him toward the ticket window.

As the crew scrambled to keep up, the crowd scattered. "See ya later, Chas!" Jesse hollered. "Don't spill any cola on your fancy new threads!"

Frodo clutched Jesse's arm. "Oh, not cola—it's only designer water for our Chas!"

Snickering and elbowing each other in the ribs, the two guys sauntered off.

Riley breathed a sigh of relief. She just hoped that the two comedians wouldn't be waiting outside when the movie was over.

"Oh, whoa!" Charlie said, scanning the movie titles. "I didn't know *Splintered* was playing here!"

[**Riley:** Oops, neither did I. *Splintered* is an indie flick about some friends trying to make it in the music business without selling out, whatever that means. I think they have lots of arguments and eventually break up. I guess you could say they *splinter*. Anyway, it's a major hit with the alternative crowd and Charlie's been dying to see it.]

"*Splintered* sounds like the *old* Charlie's pick," Dash Gilford said, stepping up next to the window. The girl in the ticket booth beamed at the camera. "But as you know, part of the makeover is doing things that go with your new look. And I'm guessing *Splintered* doesn't fit the bill."

Riley nodded. "Dash is right. *Splintered* is totally alternative. The new California Cool Charlie would never choose it. We're going to see *The Greenstone Trilogy, Part One: Hidden Fire*."

Charlie made a sound.

Riley stared at him. "Did you just pretend to gag?"

"Who, me?" He put on an innocent face. "No way. Actually, I was grinding my teeth."

Riley nodded. "I knew I heard something."

"When I gag, you'll know it," Charlie told her. "It will probably happen in the middle of *The Greenstone Trilogy*."

Riley gave him a sly grin. "Then I'd better not buy you any popcorn!"

"You tell him, Riley," Dash said.

As Riley paid for the tickets, a girl's voice squealed, "Charlie? Charlie *Slater*?"

Riley turned around. Oh, no. It was Lily, Charlie's former girlfriend. His former very *punk* girlfriend— magenta hair, black denim, multiple ear, nose, and finger rings. The guy she was with could have been her twin, except he sported a blue-tipped Mohawk. They were holding hands, so Riley figured this was Lily's new boyfriend.

Riley heard Charlie take in a deep breath. Then he plastered on a big smile. "Hi, Lily," Charlie said.

"It *is* you!" Lily looked him up and down, her eyes huge. "Whoa, this is unreal! You look so different. What happened?"

"Aw, don't tell me you haven't been watching *Total Teen Makeover*!" Dash chimed in.

"Huh?" For the first time Lily seemed to notice the camera. "What's going on?"

Dash and the crew laughed. "Well, Lily, you're on television!" Dash said, quickly explaining the situation.

It didn't seem to matter to Lily that she was on TV. She just kept staring at Charlie. "You're competing on a *makeover* show? *You?* I don't believe it!"

"Hey, why not?" Charlie asked. He shifted into an exaggerated modeling pose. Then he laughed. "What's the matter, you don't like my new look?"

Lily gave him another once-over. "You look like every other California guy."

"Yeah, that's the point," Charlie told her, relaxing again. "Just call me Chas."

"What?" Lily looked completely confused.

"Kidding," Charlie mumbled.

Hmm. He seems like he just stopped having fun, Riley thought. "Hey, it's almost time for the movie," she said, jumping in. "I guess we'd better go in."

"Oh, sure," Lily said. She nudged her boyfriend. "Erik and I saw it yesterday, and we just had to see it again. It'll blow you away!"

"*The Greenstone Trilogy?*" Riley said. "Yeah, it's supposed to be awesome."

"No, I meant *Splintered*," Lily said scornfully. "You're seeing *Greenstone?*"

Riley nodded. Charlie just looked down at his shoes.

"Oh. Well. Anything for TV, I guess." Lily gave Charlie a disgusted look and stepped up to the ticket window with Erik.

"Did you hear that?" Charlie muttered as he and

Riley walked toward the movie entrance. "She all but called me a sellout."

"Come on, forget it," Riley told him.

"I can't. I'm starting to *feel* like a sellout," he grumbled. "I mean, *The Greenstone Trilogy*?"

Riley stopped walking. "What's the matter with it?" she asked, feeling a teensy bit annoyed. "You've never even seen it."

"And I never wanted to," he said. "It's one of those superhyped Hollywood blockbusters."

"It's supposed to be awesome!" Riley argued.

"Yeah—awesomely lightweight."

Riley started to shoot something back—and suddenly remembered the television camera, which was focused on her and Charlie! So were Dash and the crew, all smiling and enjoying the little scene.

[Riley: Is this embarrassing or what? I mean, Charlie and I disagree all the time, about pretty much everything. But the television audience doesn't know that. And they're the ones who vote!]

Taking a deep breath, Riley put on a happy face and laughed as if Charlie had just said the funniest thing in the world.

chapter
five

Chloe trotted up the deck steps to her house on Sunday afternoon feeling clearheaded and calm. Dad was right, she thought. A walk on the beach beats frenzied activity every time. Really reduces the stress level.

Not that Chloe was feeling much stress. But sometimes the old Chloe would pop up and try to nudge her back to her former ways. Like earlier, when Manuelo was reading up on *faux* painting and shuffling little square paint samples all over the kitchen table, Chloe felt a strong urge to join in. Which wouldn't be so bad, except for one thing—she wouldn't just join in, she'd take charge!

But a mind-cleansing stroll took care of the old Chloe. Now the new, improved Chloe would walk right past Manuelo and the paint project without a twinge.

Sliding open the deck door, Chloe stepped into the kitchen. The books and paint samples were still there, but Manuelo wasn't. Instead, Amanda Gray, one of Chloe's best friends, sat at the table with her chin in her hands and a spiral notebook open in front of her.

"Amanda, hi!" Chloe said, surprised to see her.

"Oh, good, you're back." Amanda smiled and tucked a strand of shiny brown hair behind one ear. "I was worried that you had forgotten. Ready to study?"

[Chloe: Wow, I totally blanked on this! Not tomorrow's science test—*that's* carved into my brain. But I *did* forget that Amanda and I made plans to study for it together today. How could I do that? Oh, right. It's on my computer planner, which I haven't looked at in days!]

"Sure, let's do it," Chloe said. She grabbed a bottle of water from the refrigerator. "Want some? It's from this tiny spring in Oregon, and it's totally pure."

Amanda shook her head. "I'll take a Coke."

"Okay, but it's loaded with caffeine," Chloe warned. "It'll make you jittery."

"I'm already jittery," Amanda declared. "I'm nervous about the test. I really need to get a B or my average will drop, like, a whole grade point."

Chloe frowned. Amanda was a very logical, calm person. She didn't get upset easily. If she admitted she was nervous, what she really meant was, I'm *totally freaking*!

"Don't worry, you'll be prepared," Chloe said. "But first let's get focused."

"What do you mean?" Amanda stared at the science notes in front of her. "I *am* focused—I'm totally, completely, and thoroughly focused on the test!"

Chloe shook her head. "You're too nervous to really focus. First you have to empty your mind. *Then* you can concentrate. Come on, I'll show you."

Leading Amanda into the living room, Chloe explained her new, low-stress approach to life. "I can't believe how great it makes me feel. Taking walks, meditating, getting into yoga—it's amazing! You'll see what I mean. I'll teach you some yoga postures, and you'll feel totally relaxed."

"Well, but I really think we should study now," Amanda said doubtfully. "I'll relax *after* the test."

"But you'll do better if you aren't all tense *before*," Chloe told her. "Besides, this won't take long. Now, sit on the rug, get comfortable, and take a deep breath."

Half an hour later Amanda sighed as she struggled to get into the Full Lotus position. "I thought you said this wouldn't take long. Besides, I'll never be able to do this one!"

"Yeah, the Full Lotus is a killer," Chloe agreed. "I can get there, but I can't hold it yet. I'm still doing the Half Lotus." Crossing her legs, Chloe pulled her right foot onto her left thigh. Instead of trying to get her left foot onto her right thigh, she just tucked it under. "See? Try it this way."

Amanda managed the Half Lotus, but had trouble

keeping her back straight. And her foot kept sliding off her leg.

"Ugh!" She groaned, finally flinging her legs straight out in front of her. "Face it, I'm just not a pretzel."

"Okay, but you did the Half Moon and the Thunderbolt really well," Chloe said encouragingly.

"Maybe," Amanda said doubtfully. "But all this twisting and turning sure doesn't make me feel relaxed."

"Just keep practicing and it will," Chloe assured her. "And don't forget the breathing. That's super important."

"Chloe, I hardly ever forget to breathe," Amanda said. She stood up. "*Now* can we study?"

Back in the kitchen Amanda drank Coke and Chloe sipped spring water while they went over their class notes and quizzed each other on cell structure and the life cycle of flowering plants. Twenty minutes after they started, Amanda's mother arrived to pick her up.

"We didn't study nearly enough!" Amanda fretted as she headed for the door. "Now I have to go to this big family thing!"

"Can't you study after?"

"I guess. . . ." Amanda shrugged.

"So, no problem," Chloe said. "I'll see you tomorrow. And remember—don't stress! Relaxation helps the brain."

As Chloe shut the door, her mother hurried in from her office, looking frazzled. "What's the matter, Mom?"

"Tedi doesn't think she looks good in the green

evening gown." Macy sighed and refilled her coffee cup. "That's all I need—one of my models arguing with me!"

Dumping three spoonfuls of sugar into her mug, Macy rushed out of the kitchen.

Chloe knew her mom would talk Tedi into that green dress. They both had minds of their own, but Macy was more stubborn. Besides, they were friends. Not to mention that Mom was the boss.

Still, just thinking about the whole thing gave Chloe a twinge of anxiety. She was one of the models, too. She knew what these presentations were like—total chaos, with lots of rushing around, last minute Velcro taping of hems, and superhurried changes of clothes. Talk about stress!

Exactly what I don't want right now, Chloe thought. But what could she do? Mom was counting on her.

Or, she suddenly realized, on somebody *like* her!

Riley headed for the school radio studio on Monday morning, eager to do the show. *Total Makeover* would be filming her and Charlie "at work" today, and she just knew it would be great. No heckling from Frodo and Jesse, and no surprise appearances by a former girlfriend.

Just Charlie and me having fun, she thought. Like we usually do.

Rounding the corner, Riley spotted Charlie and Sierra standing together outside the studio door. Standing *very close* together. Practically huddling, actually.

Riley stared at them curiously. The conversation looked extremely intense. What could they be talking about?

"Hi, guys," Riley called as she walked toward them. "What's up?"

Stepping quickly away from Sierra, Charlie gave Riley a wave and ducked into the studio.

"What was that all about?" Riley asked Sierra as her friend hurried toward her.

"I was just telling Charlie how great he looks," Sierra said. She peered over Riley's shoulder into the studio. "He . . . whoa!" Her eyes widened. "Is that the time? I've got to get to class. Oh," she added as she turned away, "the television crew is already in the studio. So smile!"

"Thanks." Riley went into the studio, squeezed past Dave and his camera, and plopped into the chair beside Charlie's. "Hi," she said.

"Hey." Charlie gave her a quick smile and went back to shuffling CDs around.

[Riley: Uh-oh. That smile lasted all of a nano-second. Something's wrong.]

"What's the matter?" Riley whispered.

Charlie shook his head.

"Okay, is everybody ready?" Dash asked. Dave and the crew nodded. "Riley and Charlie, take it away!"

Riley turned on her studio mike. "Hey, West Malibu High!" she said. "Welcome to *The Morning Rant!*"

"Or rather, *Morning Pop Chart*," Charlie said into his mike.

Riley laughed. "In case you don't know, Charlie and I are appearing on *Total Teen Makeover*. In fact"—she swiveled in her seat and waved at a camera, then swiveled back—"we're being filmed right this very moment. So today Charlie will choose music to go with his new look. What will Mr. California Cool play, Charlie?"

Charlie rolled his eyes. "ABP. Anything But Punk. Unfortunately."

"You got that right." Riley laughed. "So what's it going to be?"

"Gee, Riley, there's just so much great stuff to choose from, I can't decide," Charlie said. "Why don't you pick the first piece?"

"Ooo-kay, I will," Riley chirped, ignoring Charlie's sarcastic tone. "Let's start off with something from Caleb."

"Caleb, huh?" Charlie said. "Can you hear my teeth grinding?"

"Yep, and I'm sure the whole school can, too," Riley said. "Try not to drown out the music."

She punched the button and turned off their microphones. "Okay, what's wrong?" she asked. "Did Frodo and Jesse dis you again?"

"Of course they did. But that's not the problem,"

Charlie told her. "The problem is I still haven't heard from the manager at K-SUN about that weekend job."

Riley felt relieved. Charlie wasn't mad at *her*. "But that's good actually," she assured him. "It means he hasn't decided yet, so you still have a chance."

Charlie frowned as he nodded. "Right. You're right." He shifted in his chair. "The seams in this shirt itch," he said, tugging at the fitted mushroom-colored shirt. He pulled the ends of his hair. "And my hair feels weird. I liked it better long."

"Well, Charlie, I've got good news for you," Riley said. "Hair grows back."

Charlie held up his hands as if he were calling a truce. "Okay, okay. I know this is all part of my new image. Like playing pop music instead of the good stuff."

Now Riley rolled her eyes. "Punk isn't the only good music in the world. You know that. And I really don't get why you're so grumpy. The makeover show will be over in a few days, and you can revert to your old self. What's the big deal?"

[Riley: Yikes! *The makeover show*! I forgot about the camera—again! They're getting all of this on tape.]

Riley turned in her chair. Dave, Dash, and the others were grinning at her and Charlie, just the way they had at the cineplex.

"Don't stop because of us, you two," Dash urged.

"Just pretend we're not here. A good spat is always fun."

For you, maybe, Riley thought. But not for me. And not if we want to win the contest.

The cut ended. Riley turned away from the camera, ready to do the usual in-between-tunes bantering with Charlie. But Charlie just silently slipped in a new CD and punched it on, then leaned his head back and closed his eyes.

What is the *matter* with him? Riley wondered. But this time she didn't ask. Vowing that she'd never forget the camera again, she pasted on a smile and pretended she was having a great time.

When Riley headed for the Newsstand later that afternoon, she was feeling much better. She figured Charlie would be in a better mood, too. In spite of his doom-and-gloom punk appearance, he was basically an upbeat guy.

He just needed to vent, I guess, Riley thought. Everybody does. The past few days *had* been pretty intense. But there were only two more sessions with the television crew. They were scheduled for a restaurant date on Wednesday. Then, on Friday, they'd be filmed in a "surprise" segment, which Dash Gilford would announce at the last minute.

As she approached the Newsstand, Riley peered through the front window—and spotted Charlie and Sierra inside the café.

Her boyfriend and her best friend were near the coffee bar. They were hunched over a small table with their heads almost touching as they carried on an extremely intense conversation.

Another one.

Riley quickly stepped away from the window.

[Riley: **Don't you hate feeling suspicious? Me, too. But right now I can't help it! Sierra really wanted Charlie and me to enter the contest. She was positive Charlie would turn out to be a real hottie. Now she keeps saying his new look blows her away. Was she crushing on him even before the contest? And what about Charlie? He's a total grouch with me, but he has plenty of time for major head-to-heads with Sierra! Is he falling for her?]**

Walking on past the Newsstand, Riley told herself to get a grip. Sierra and Charlie? It couldn't be true! Could it?

chapter
six

"**I**t *could* be true, couldn't it?" Riley asked Chloe later that afternoon. "I mean, it's possible!"

The sisters were sprawled on the floor in Chloe's bedroom, sharing a pint of frozen raspberry yogurt, discussing the Charlie/Sierra question.

[**Riley**: It's our crisis-control method. Got a problem? Grab two spoons and talk. Usually we talk over ice cream, but with Chloe's new meditation-and-millet lifestyle, we opted for the yogurt.]

"Well, I don't believe it, and neither should you," Chloe declared, dipping her spoon into the yogurt. "Riley, Sierra is your best friend. She wouldn't go after Charlie."

Riley's forehead crinkled. "You think?" she said hopefully.

Chloe nodded. "And don't forget—Charlie loves you!"

[**Riley**: Yeah, he does. . . . Well, he did. Does he still?]

"Aha!" Chloe cried, pointing her spoon at Riley. "Negative thoughts. I can see them on your face!"

Riley stopped biting her lip and managed a smile. "You're right. I can't help it."

"Yes, you can!" Chloe insisted. "You should do some yoga with me. It'll help get rid of all those negative feelings. Really!"

Riley smiled again but shook her head. "The only way to get rid of *these* negative feelings is to find out the truth," she said. "But I'm afraid to ask." She shivered. "What if I *am* right? Talk about negative feelings!"

"You're *not* right," Chloe insisted.

Riley let out a big, long sigh. "Well, I sure would like to be wrong."

"Remember," Chloe added, "I know all kinds of de-stressing exercises. And they work. Promise you'll let me show you if you change your mind?"

"I promise," Riley said. "I mean, I can tell they work. You're so mellow, I'm getting sleepy just being with you." She grinned. "Kidding," she said, licking her spoon.

Chloe laughed but then became serious. "Listen, I hate to ask, with your being upset and all, but I need a favor."

"Sure. What?" Riley asked.

"It's about Mom's new fashion presentation on

Saturday." Chloe explained that she didn't want to model because it would be so hectic and she was working really hard not to get involved in stressful situations. "So would you take my place?" she asked. "I already checked with Mom, and she's cool with it, if you are."

"Sure. I'll do it," Riley agreed. "I had fun when I did it before."

Chloe gave her a hug. "Riley, thank you! I'll pay you back, I promise. The next time you need a favor, I'm there!"

Riley hugged her sister back. They didn't keep tabs on favors. She knew her sister would *always* be there for her.

But she couldn't help wondering—would Charlie?

"How are the dance plans going?" Chloe asked, standing with Tara and Quinn in the cafeteria line on Tuesday. "What theme did you come up with?"

Tara frowned. "We already told you. *Moonlight Rocks*."

"Oh, I like that," Chloe said. Then she blinked. "Wait—you told me?"

Quinn nodded. "We also told you what music to burn on the CDs."

Chloe plunked a triple-pepper wrap onto her tray. "Why don't I don't remember this?"

"I have a better question," Tara said. "Why don't you answer your e-mails?"

"Oh!" Chloe nodded as she suddenly saw the light.

"You e-mailed me about the CDs and the theme? That explains everything."

"Is your computer down?" Tara asked sympathetically.

"No, nothing like that," Chloe explained. "I've only been using it for schoolwork." She sighed contentedly. "It's so peaceful not being online all the time. You guys should try it."

"Are you kidding? I'd go nuts," Quinn declared.

"Me, too," Tara agreed. "Anyway, since you didn't read our e-mails, I'm guessing you haven't burned any CDs. Am I right?"

[Chloe: I get the feeling Tara's a tiny bit ticked off. Maybe this isn't the best time to suggest yoga.]

"You're right," Chloe said. "I'll check the e-mails when I get home. And don't stress, okay? The dance is still days away."

"True," Tara said. "But we want to make sure everything comes together just right. You know how it is."

Chloe laughed. "I definitely know how it is. That's why I decided to chill."

"Since when does *chill* equal *drop out*?" Quinn complained. "You never IM anybody. We hardly even see you anymore!"

"Well, we're together now, right?" Chloe said, taking some orange juice. "Let's find a table and catch up."

"We can't," Tara said. "We have a dance committee meeting. We're all eating in one of the study halls. We'll try to find you later."

Quinn and Tara left with their food, and Chloe took her tray to one of the tables. She sat down and saw Amanda coming toward her with an extremely unhappy expression on her face. She stopped at Chloe's table.

"Amanda? What's wrong?" Chloe asked.

"I got a C on the science test." Amanda's voice sounded thick, as if she might cry. "C as in *crummy*!"

"Oh, Amanda, I'm sorry!" Chloe said. She'd gotten a B, but she decided that was another thing it was better not to mention.

"I should have studied harder," Amanda wailed. "I shouldn't have wasted all that time trying to twist myself into a pretzel."

Uh-oh. Is Amanda mad at me for trying to help her relax? Chloe worried.

Amanda bit her lip. "Don't worry, I'm not blaming you, Chloe," she said, as if she could read Chloe's mind. "It's my fault. I let you talk me into it."

"But you knew the stuff we studied," Chloe said.

"And I even studied that night," Amanda said. "But the minute I saw the test, I freaked."

Chloe nodded sympathetically. "I've done that, too. But really, Amanda, all you need is more practice."

Amanda looked confused. "Practice test-taking?"

"No, no. Yoga, relaxation," Chloe said. "Just keep

doing the exercises, and you'll never freak again."

Amanda rolled her eyes. "Thanks, but I think I'll just study harder. In fact, I'm going to see if I can do some extra-credit work to help my average. Talk to you later."

Chloe watched Amanda hurry out of the cafeteria and sighed. She felt bad for Amanda and wished she could help.

When she's not so upset, I'll talk to her again about de-stressing, she decided, taking a bite of her wrap. That'll definitely help. All I have to do is get her to believe me.

"Hey, Chloe," Lennon said, coming up to the table.

"Lennon!" Chloe half stood and gave him a kiss. "What are you doing here?"

"They're fixing some lights in the gym, so they kicked us out for a few minutes," Lennon explained. "We came to get something to drink." He gestured toward his friends, Morgan and Rick, who were at one of the vending machines.

"Anyway, I wanted to talk to you about my grandmother," he said.

"Oh, right!" Chloe said. "When am I going to meet her?"

"Is tomorrow after school okay?" Lennon asked. "She wants us to have afternoon tea at some new tearoom. I know, it sounds boring, but what can I do?"

"But I'm really into tea now," Chloe said. "It'll be fun."

"Fun?" Lennon repeated. "You don't know Grand-mother."

"Oh?"

Lennon laughed. "Don't get me wrong. She's great and everything, but she's pretty particular about things. Like clothes and food and dust and air-conditioning and manners—you want me to go on?"

"I get the picture." Chloe laughed. "Don't worry. I won't wear a micromini or slurp my tea."

Lennon laughed, too. "Cool." He gave her a quick kiss.

Chloe wished he could stay. She was just about to suggest that they get together later when his friends came up and reminded him that they were going biking after school.

Lennon said good-bye, and the guys hurried out of the cafeteria, laughing and talking about biking trails and gear.

Chloe suddenly felt left out. Everybody was doing something, and she was alone with a soggy pepper wrap.

Don't be ridiculous, she told herself. Nobody excluded you on purpose.

Taking a cleansing breath to banish the negative feeling, Chloe picked up the wrap and finished her lunch.

chapter
seven

"**M**mm!" Riley mumbled, her mouth full of chipotle salsa and chips. "Is this great or what?"

"It's okay," Charlie said, reaching for his water glass.

It was Wednesday, and they were at Amadeo's, having a dinner date. If you can call it a "date" with the *Total Teen Makeover* crew along, filming their next-to-last segment, Riley thought.

[Riley: Sigh. I picked this place because Charlie loves Mexican food—the spicier, the better. But between you and me, the salsa is pretty bland, and Charlie's barely said two words to me.]

Remembering her vow to smile no matter what, Riley kept the corners of her mouth turned way up. But Charlie was definitely bummed. Was it the clothes? The camera? *Sierra*?

Riley hesitated. Should she ask what was wrong?

Yes, she decided. She cared about him, and it was obvious that something was bothering him.

Her heart skipped a beat. What if it's about Sierra? He wouldn't break up with me on camera, would he?

Charlie just stared at the chips as if he were counting them.

Well, this silence isn't going to help us win the contest, Riley thought. Or bring us back closer together again.

"Hey, Charlie, what's wrong?" Riley asked softly. She really hated to have this conversation in front of the TV crew, but she didn't feel as if she had a choice.

Charlie didn't even look up. "I didn't get the job," he said quietly.

He meant the part-time DJ job at K-SUN, Riley realized. The one he really, really wanted.

"The manager listened to us on the day I had to play that pop stuff," Charlie went on. "He didn't like what he heard. He said I wouldn't fit in at K-SUN."

"That's ridiculous," Riley declared indignantly. "If anybody fits in at an alternative radio station, it's you. Did you explain what was going on?"

"I didn't get a chance," Charlie said. "He had four calls waiting."

Glancing at the camera, Riley forced herself to keep smiling. Maybe she could joke him out of his bad mood. "I think we should find the guy and dump this bowl of salsa on his head."

Charlie gave her a *get real* look.

"Just kidding." Riley laughed. "You know me, always kidding around." Which wasn't true, but the television audience didn't need to know that. "Let's see. . . . Oh! We could picket the station. Yeah! A protest, with chants and signs and everything. 'Hire Charlie Slater! Or it's later, alligator!'"

Charlie rolled his eyes.

"Okay, that was kind of feeble," Riley admitted.

"Kind of," Charlie agreed, snapping a chip in half.

Riley's cheeks were starting to ache from smiling so hard. She knew she must look like a total airhead. But it was important to at least *pretend* to be cheerful. The happiest couple wins the contest—didn't Charlie get that? She had to get him to laugh. Or at least *smile*!

Riley dunked a chip into the salsa and munched while she tried to think of something wacko enough to make Charlie crack a smile. "I've got it!" she declared. "Skywriting! We get an airplane to buzz over K-SUN's studio and write a message."

"Riley . . ."

"Can you see it?" Riley went on, grinning frantically. "K-SUN N*eeds Slater*. But catchier. What rhymes with Slater? Later, cater, waiter. Or Charlie—barley, gnarly . . ."

"Riley . . ."

"No good? Okay, rhyming's out." Not even a *hint* of a smile on his face. In fact, he was starting to sound seriously annoyed.

Riley desperately gave it another try. "Want to go back to the salsa on the head? Guacamole instead?" She laughed loudly.

"Riley, stop!" Charlie said.

Riley took a breath.

"Quit joking around, okay?" he said. "I know you're trying to cheer me up, but I'm really steamed!"

[Riley: It's true. The smoke's practically coming out of his ears—and it's not because of the salsa!]

"Well, I don't blame you," Riley told him. "Who wouldn't be steamed? K-SUN made a major mistake!"

"No, I did!" Charlie said. He waved a hand toward the camera. "Going along with this stupid makeover thing—*that* was the mistake! Wearing dumb clothes and seeing dumb movies and playing dumb music! That's why I didn't get the job. I never should have let you talk me into it."

"What do you say to that, Riley?" Dash Gilford called from his spot next to the camera.

Riley glanced at the TV host. He had a big smile on his face. So did Miri and Dave. They were obviously enjoying the mini-drama. It's as if they *want* us to argue, she thought.

Riley threw Dash and the crew a fake grin and turned back to Charlie. "Come on," she said, trying to figure out how to save the situation. "The man from

K-SUN didn't see your clothes, and he didn't know you went to *The Greenstone Trilogy*. So don't blame the makeover show." Or me, she added silently. But she didn't want to say that on camera.

"She's got a point, Charlie!" Dash called.

Charlie ignored him. "I *know* he didn't see me," he told Riley. "But he heard all that junk music I was playing, remember?"

"Playing that so-called junk music was part of the makeover," she said, scowling at Charlie. "The makeover *you* said you'd go along with."

"Yeah, well, I must have been totally nuts," he declared. "I never should have said yes."

"But you did," Riley told him heatedly.

"Please. Don't remind me."

Riley felt like dumping the salsa on *Charlie's* head, but she controlled herself. "I can't believe you're being such a bad sport about this. This was supposed to be fun, and you're spoiling the whole thing. It's totally ridiculous!"

"So's this makeover deal," Charlie shot back.

"Well, it's almost finished!" Riley snapped.

"She's right about that, Charlie!" Dash announced, joining them at the table.

Omigosh! Riley had gotten so mad at Charlie, she'd totally forgotten about the camera! They'd just had a major blowout for the entire television audience to watch!

"There's only one more segment to go!" Dash said. "Are you kids ready to hear about it, or should we wait until the fight's over? Ha-ha!"

Ha-ha, Riley thought, feeling her cheeks burning. "I'm ready to hear about it," she said. She glanced at Charlie.

Charlie nodded. "Fine."

"All right!" Dash grinned and gleefully rubbed his hands together. "Charlie, I think you're going to like this. For your final segment, we're turning the tables. And *you* get to be in charge! You pick the place—and you pick the look! How does that sound?"

Charlie seemed to perk up a little. "You mean I can wear what I want?"

"Well, no," Dash said. "You'll still be in your California Cool duds." Then he winked at Charlie. "But here's the part you'll like. For your final *Total Teen Makeover* date, *Riley* will get the makeover!"

[Riley: Uh-oh. Charlie has perked *way* up. What am I in for? This is his chance to get back at me.]

"So what'll it be, Charlie?" Dash asked. "Where do you want to go, and what kind of look do you pick for Riley?"

"That's easy," Charlie told Dash. "There's this new alternative club called Xtreme opening on Friday." He leaned back in his chair, a grin slowly spreading across his face. His brown eyes twinkled at Riley. "You can probably guess what to wear."

[Riley: Duh. I bet the whole TV audience can guess what Charlie will want me to wear.]

"Gee," Riley said, smiling so hard that her cheeks started aching again. "How about something . . . punk!"

chapter eight

On Thursday after school Chloe went home and changed into a rose-colored top and a short, but not *too* short, skirt. Then she headed back out to meet Lennon and his grandmother at Teatime.

Glancing toward the Newsstand as she strolled along, Chloe saw a bunch of kids heading into the café. Tara and Quinn, Sam, Rudy, Margot . . . it was the entire dance committee. Chloe waved, but nobody was looking in her direction.

"Anybody got any money?" she heard Sam holler, reaching for the door. "I went a little crazy buying CDs this month."

"Again?" Quinn laughed, following him. "I guess we can scrape together enough to buy you a cappuccino."

"Yeah, you deserve it after putting up all those silver streamers in the gym," Tara agreed.

"I say that rates a cappuccino *and* a muffin!" Sam

joked. He pushed open the door, and the group piled inside.

They must have been working on the decorations, Chloe realized. Now they've decided to kick back.

Chloe stopped and peered into the front window. Everyone was bunched around the coffee counter. She couldn't hear them, but she could tell they were razzing Sam—probably about spending all his money on CDs. And Rudy was showing Margot some kind of funky dance step.

Chloe couldn't help wishing she was with them. Well, why not go in? she decided. Then she caught sight of the clock over the counter.

Yikes. She was already ten minutes late for tea with Lennon and his grandmother!

Hurrying away from the Newsstand, Chloe wondered how she could possibly be late. Maybe the clock was wrong? She started to check her watch but then remembered she'd stopped wearing it. She'd also stopped carrying her cell phone, so she couldn't check the time on that.

As she approached Teatime, a quaint little shop that looked like an English cottage, Chloe told herself not to stress. Lennon said his grandmother was really great. This is going to be fun! Besides, if I'm late, it's only a few minutes. What's the big deal?

Taking a deep, calming breath, Chloe pushed open the door and stepped inside. She spotted Lennon immediately. He sat at one of the round tables covered with a lace cloth. With him was a tall, older woman with her silvery hair in a stylish short cut.

Uh-oh. They were both looking at their watches.

"Lennon, hi!" Chloe said, hurrying across the room. "You must be Lennon's grandmother," she added. "I'm really glad to meet you."

Mrs. Porter smiled. "I'm glad to meet you, too, Chloe."

"Finally," Lennon said under his breath.

Chloe could tell he was slightly annoyed. "I'm sorry I'm late. I guess I lost track of the time!"

"I hope you don't mind, but we already ordered," Mrs. Porter said.

"No, that's great." Chloe sat down and glanced around at the beamed ceiling and the teapots used for decoration. "What a cute place."

"Isn't it? I hope the tea's good," Mrs. Porter said. "It should have been here by now." She checked her watch and glanced around in search of a waiter.

"Grandmother has to be somewhere else in half an hour," Lennon explained to Chloe.

"I hate rushing," Mrs. Porter said. "Tea should be savored, not rushed."

"Oh, definitely," Chloe agreed. She glanced at Lennon, who was frowning at the tablecloth. Well, he had said his grandmother was particular. Now she knew what he meant.

The waiter arrived with a pot of jasmine green tea and a three-tiered tray containing scones and jam, butter cookies, and no-crust sandwiches the size of credit cards.

"This looks great!" Chloe said.

Mrs. Porter surveyed the spread. "I believe we ordered clotted cream," she told the waiter. She frowned slightly as he hurried off. "I hope it's fresh."

"I wouldn't know if it wasn't fresh," Chloe admitted. "I don't even know what it is."

[Chloe: It turns out to be cream that's gotten really thick so it's sort of like soft butter. You put it on a scone, then you plop on some jam. While Mrs. Porter told me about it, Lennon polished off six mini-sandwiches.]

The cream arrived. "It tastes best if the scones are hot, but we don't have time to get them reheated," Mrs. Porter complained. She shook her head, then turned to Chloe. "So, Chloe, tell me what you're up to these days. Lennon says you're always juggling a dozen different things, up to your ears in projects."

"I used to be," Chloe said, slathering some of the cream onto a scone. "But I was getting way too stressed. Plus I never had time to just chill. Now I'm doing yoga and meditation, and I'm *so* much more relaxed. It's great! I'd be glad to tell you about it."

Lennon nudged Chloe's arm. "I don't think Grandmother's into yoga and stuff."

"Neither was I!" Chloe said. "But it really, really works. See, when you know all the little tricks to de-stress, then things like the cream and the cooled-off scones just don't matter."

Another nudge from Lennon.

"I mean, they *matter*," Chloe tried to explain. She didn't want Lennon's grandmother to think she was insulting her! "But you don't let them get to you. Of course," she added, staring at her scone, "cream's not the best thing for stress. Veganism is supposed to be great for you."

"Veganism?" Mrs. Porter repeated.

"That's a diet of just plants. No animal products, not even dairy," Chloe explained just as Mrs. Porter bit into her cream-topped scone.

Another nudge from Lennon.

[Chloe: Oops!]

"*Anyway*, it's not just food," Chloe added. "You have to decide what's really important and only worry about that."

"I thought you weren't supposed to worry at all," Lennon commented.

"Well, *that's* impossible. Everybody worries," Chloe told him. She turned back to Mrs. Porter. But Lennon's grandmother was rummaging through her purse and eyeing her watch.

[Chloe: Hmm. I get the feeling she's not interested in de-stressing. I also get the feeling that

if I say one more word about it, Lennon's going to nudge me off my chair!]

Mrs. Porter excused herself and headed for the ladies' room.

"I got kind of carried away, didn't I?" Chloe said to Lennon.

"Kind of," he agreed.

[Chloe: Ouch. I was hoping he'd say, "No, you were perfect."]

"I didn't mean to blab so much," Chloe admitted. "I just like to talk about my new lifestyle, that's all."

"Uh-huh." Lennon drummed his fingers on the table.

"Okay, what's the matter?" she asked. "Are you mad because I was late? Did your grandmother bug you about it?"

"She wasn't angry that you were late, exactly. But she definitely noticed. So why *were* you?"

"Because . . ." Chloe shrugged. "I don't know. Don't tell me *you're* mad because I was late."

"Well, Chloe, it's kind of rude."

[Chloe: Ouch again.]

"I'm sorry," Chloe said. "You're right." She looked at Lennon, expecting a smile, but he still looked serious. "Is . . . is something else wrong?"

"Well . . . things aren't any different. I thought this

whole de-stress thing was supposed to give us some more time together. I still never see you."

"That's not true," Chloe said. "I've just been learning how to relax. You wanted me to chill, right?"

"Yeah, chill," Lennon agreed. "Not disappear."

Mrs. Porter returned and they left the shop and said their good-byes. Lennon gave Chloe a quick kiss, but she could tell he was still unhappy with the way the meeting went.

Chloe tried not to think about the mini-argument with Lennon as she walked home. She took lots of deep breaths, but all they did was make her mouth dry. She needed something else to focus on.

Aha! Up ahead was the Newsstand. She'd have a decaf soymilk latte with Tara and Quinn and the rest of the dance committee. That would take her mind off Lennon.

Passing the café's front window, Chloe eagerly peered inside.

The dance committee was gone. She checked out the tables. There were plenty of kids, but nobody she knew very well.

Okay, new plan. She'd go home and do some yoga, light some candles, and take a long bath.

Picking up her pace, Chloe hurried home and trotted upstairs. As she kicked off her shoes, she eyed the blank computer monitor across the room. It seemed like forever since she'd used it for anything but homework. Who knew how many e-mails she'd missed?

Chloe flicked on the computer.

Oh, good! She'd gotten e-mails from Tara and Quinn. No, wait—those were old e-mails. The ones they'd sent about burning the CDs.

Was that *all*?

It must be a mistake, Chloe thought. She closed the program and opened it again. The same two e-mails showed up. That *was* all.

Well, as long as she was online, why not chat with somebody? She brought up her buddy list and checked the screen names for Tara, Quinn, Amanda, Lennon, even Larry next door. But no one was around to chat with her.

Where *was* everybody?

As Chloe was frowning at the screen, Riley burst into the room. "Remember when I said I'd model for you in Mom's presentation?" Riley said breathlessly. "And you said you'd pay me back?"

Chloe nodded. "Let me guess—it's payback time?"

"You got it," Riley told her. Flopping down onto Chloe's bed, she described the surprise makeover she'd be going through tomorrow.

Chloe laughed. "Punk? Don't worry, Riley. You look good in black."

Riley rolled her eyes. "What about tattoos and nose rings?"

"No way!" Chloe cried.

"Fake," Riley assured her. "Anyway, after I get the

clothes and stuff, they're going to do *something* with my hair. And how's this for a kicker?"

"You have to sing?" Chloe joked.

"Worse!" Riley moaned. "I've been challenged to do my own makeup. They'll provide me with all the Goth colors, and it's up to me to use them."

"What do you want me to do?" Chloe asked. "I'm not exactly the Goth type either."

"But you're better with makeup than I am," Riley pointed out. "You might actually manage to make me look less like a freak. No matter how much I'll feel like one."

Chloe laughed. "I'll do my best. When do we do your makeover?"

"I refuse to turn alternative until I absolutely have to, right before we head out to the club. So I guess . . . five-fifteen?"

"I'll be here," Chloe promised. "It'll be fun."

"For you, maybe," Riley griped. "Anyway, thanks, Chloe."

"No problem," Chloe said. And she meant it. It *would* be fun. And having something to look forward to was kind of fun, too.

In fact, Chloe realized, putting the makeup appointment on her mental schedule made her feel a whole lot better.

chapter
nine

"**W**ell, Riley, what do you think?" Dash Gilford asked on Friday afternoon. "How do you like the look?"

> [<u>Riley</u>: Picture this: I just came out of the dressing room of Brand X in a black mini over black tights, a short black tee with a mean-looking Day-Glo pumpkin on the back, a silver ring on every finger, and a thin piece of purple silk around my neck.]

"I like this," Riley said, fingering the purple silk.

> [<u>Riley</u>: Hey, at least it's a color!]

"Ha! Did you hear that, Charlie?" Dash laughed, elbowing Charlie in the arm. "I don't think Riley likes your taste."

Riley noticed Miri and the rest of the crew perk up. They were probably hoping for another argument. Well, they wouldn't get one from *her*. Not this time.

"I like it fine," Riley fibbed. "I just like the scarf best."

Charlie gave her a quick smile. Riley wouldn't call it *warm*, exactly, but at least he was in a better mood today. Probably because he was turning the tables on her.

"The shoes don't work," Charlie commented, staring at Riley's copper-colored sandals. "You need boots. You know, like I usually wear."

The green-haired girl who was waiting on them bustled into the storeroom and found a pair of combat boots in Riley's size. Riley put them on and laced them up.

"You're right," Riley said, clomping over to the mirror. "They go much better with the outfit." Even if they weigh at least five pounds apiece, she thought.

"Okay! Looking good!" Dash rubbed his hands together. "Now for the tattoos. Right, Charlie? And maybe a nose ring?"

"Oh, gee, we can't do tattoos here," the green-haired girl said apologetically. "There's a licensed store down the street. But we do piercings!" She pointed to the safety pin through her left eyebrow.

Riley's stomach fluttered.

"That's okay, we don't want the real thing," Charlie told her. "We just want the stick-on kind of tattoo. And not a nose ring. Maybe one of those little magnetic studs."

Smiling at the camera, the girl gestured toward the baskets on the counter. "We've got both of those!"

Riley joined Charlie at the counter. "Thanks for not wanting me to get the real thing," she murmured. "Not that my mom would let me, even if I wanted to."

[Riley: Which I don't. Not even a little.]

"No problem," Charlie said. He started shuffling through some stick-on tattoos.

Something is still off, Riley thought. He was smiling more, but things just didn't feel the same. Was he still mad and just covering up? Or was he thinking about Sierra?

No, no, no! Do not go there, Riley ordered herself.

"These are good," Charlie said, handing Riley a couple of the tattoos.

They checked out the nose studs next, and Charlie picked a tiny silver one. Then they all left Brand X and headed for a place called The Chop Shop, a hair salon for punks and punkettes.

Turner, the man in charge, sat Riley in a chair and rattled off the possibilities. "Streaked, Mohawk, spiked, shaved . . ."

[Riley: Shaved? Gulp!]

"Um . . ." Riley gave a weak laugh and gestured at Charlie. "It's up to him."

"That's right!" Dash chimed in. "What'll it be, Charlie?"

"Hmm . . ." Charlie studied Riley's straight blond hair.

Riley held her breath.

"Don't cut it or anything," Charlie said.

Whew!

"Can you just give her a funkier style?" Charlie asked.

"Sure," Turner said. "Cool."

"With some purple in it," Charlie added.

Turner smiled. "Way cool."

Maybe not *way* cool, Riley thought as she stared into the mirror thirty minutes later. Turner had moussed and gelled her hair so it lay flat against her head, then picked out several strands, colored them purple, and gelled them into spikes. Then he sprayed it until Riley's head felt encased in plastic.

[Riley: **Maybe not cool at all. I feel like I should go trick-or-treating.**]

At least the purple hair color was the kind that could be washed out. But her new weird look wasn't the real problem. The problem was between her and Charlie.

Riley sighed at her punk reflection. I thought the contest would bring us together, she thought. Instead it's breaking us apart. And if Charlie really has feelings for Sierra, then we might never be together again.

"Hi, this is Lennon," Lennon's voice mail said on Friday afternoon. "Can't talk right now, but I'll call you back, so leave a message."

At the beep Chloe said, "Hi, Lennon. It's me, Chloe. I guess you don't have your cell phone on. I just felt like talking. No big deal. Bye."

But it was a *little* deal, Chloe thought as she hung up the kitchen phone. She'd missed seeing Lennon at school today, and she wanted to make sure he wasn't still mad about the tea date. Second of all, she did want to just talk. She felt as if she'd barely had contact with anyone for a week.

Picking up the phone again, Chloe punched in Amanda's number.

"Amanda's not here, Chloe," Mrs. Gray said. "She's at the mall with Tara and Quinn. They're trying to win the one-hour shopping spree at that new boutique that opened today."

Mrs. Gray talked as if Chloe knew which boutique she meant. But Chloe didn't have a clue, which was totally unnatural for somebody who loved shopping. Of course, that was the old Chloe, she reminded herself.

"Well, I hope they win," Chloe said.

"So do they." Mrs. Gray laughed. "The prize goes to the hundredth customer to enter the store. They said they were going to stake it out and count!"

"Sounds like fun. Thanks, Mrs. Gray." Chloe hung up, smiling. She could just picture her three friends trying to keep track of all the customers. Quinn would laugh too much and lose count. Tara would try to keep count by what they wore, like *red pants* or *yellow dress*.

Amanda would probably use a calculator, which the others would tease her about. It *did* sound like fun.

Chloe sat down at the kitchen table, then popped right up again. She felt restless. She'd already done some yoga, but it hadn't seemed to help. The yoga book talked about setbacks. Maybe that's what this was. All she needed was a long walk, Chloe decided, and the antsy feeling would disappear.

As Chloe headed for the door, her mother rushed into the kitchen. Macy had her cell clapped to her ear and a look of total shock on her face. "Are you serious?" she said into the phone. "Please, tell me you're not!"

Chloe watched as Macy listened to whoever was on the other end of the phone line. What could be the problem?

"Uh-huh," Macy said. "But can't you . . . next *week*? Nothing until then? I see. All right. Well, thank you anyway. Of course. Good-bye." Macy hung up and hurled herself toward the coffeemaker on the counter.

"Mom, what happened?" Chloe asked.

Macy jumped, startled. "Chloe! I didn't see you there."

"I was just going out for a walk," Chloe explained. "What happened?"

"Oh, just a minor disaster," Macy said, pouring a mug of coffee. "Catering to Malibu had a fire. Nobody was hurt, but their kitchen was totally destroyed."

"It doesn't sound minor to me," Chloe said anxiously. "I mean, Mom! Your presentation is tomorrow!"

"Well, it'll sound minor when I tell you what happened earlier," Macy declared, stirring in sugar. "The Garden Room was double-booked. I'm out of a showroom."

"Oh, no!" Chloe cried. "What are you going to do? How can you find another place in time?"

"It's a challenge, that's for sure," Macy agreed, her voice tight. Taking her mug and a deep breath, Macy charged back to her office.

Chloe went outside and started to stroll along the beach. It was a gorgeous evening, with a soft wind and a pink sun slowly setting. Chloe tried to focus on the sunset, but her mind kept wandering back to her mother's problems.

Tromping along the beach, Chloe shook her head doubtfully. Mom had to find another caterer and another place to hold the show—and she had less than twenty-four hours to do it!

Chloe slowed down, trying to decide what to do. Should she stay out of it? Or go back and help?

As carefully as possible Riley eased the short black tee over her head and checked the mirror. Good. Her hair hadn't budged. Every purple spike was still in place. Maybe Turner really *did* use plastic!

It was a few minutes after five. The *Total Makeover* van would be here at five-forty-five. Riley was ready—clothes, hair, snake tattoo on her left arm, rose tattoo on her right collarbone, fake nose stud glinting in her left nostril. The makeup Turner gave her was laid out on her dresser. All she needed now was Chloe to help put it on.

Riley clomped downstairs to the kitchen in her thick-soled boots. Manuelo was putting something away in the refrigerator. He straightened up, saw Riley, and clutched his chest dramatically. "Ay!" he gasped. "Please! There are no jewels in the house. Maybe a little cash. Will that do?"

Riley giggled. "Come on, do I really look dangerous?"

"No. Just baaaad," Manuelo drawled. "I especially like the hair. What is *on* it? Shellac?"

"Probably." Riley heard her mother's voice from the office, talking fast. "Mom sounds kind of upset."

Manuelo nodded. "Problems with the presentation, I think. She hasn't gotten off the phone long enough to tell me."

"Oh. I hope everything works out okay," Riley said. "Listen, the television van's gonna be here soon. Have you seen Chloe?"

"Not since she got home from school."

Riley glanced at the kitchen clock. Ten after five. Not much time left. "If you see her, would you tell her I'm waiting in my room with the makeup?"

Manuelo agreed, and Riley hurried back upstairs.

At five-fifteen Riley stuck her head out the door. She heard her mother's voice on the phone again but nothing else. "Chloe?"

No answer. Where *was* she?

At five-twenty-five, Riley called downstairs again. "Manuelo?"

"Riley?"

"Mom? I thought you were on the phone."

"I just got off," Macy called out. "Manuelo went on an errand. Back in five, he said." The phone rang. "Good luck tonight, sweetie!"

"Thanks!"

Five-twenty-six.

Chloe *said* she'd be here, Riley thought anxiously. With this new lifestyle of hers, it's not as if she's got a gazillion other things going on!

Finally Riley couldn't wait any longer. She grabbed the foundation and used a little sponge to smear it all over her face. The makeup made her skin look pale, but that was the idea, Riley guessed.

Next came eye shadow. Kind of a brownish-pink. Lots of it, Turner advised, so Riley swooped on plenty. Ugh. Her eyelids looked bruised. If only Chloe were here! Her sister was the makeup wizard. She'd know what to do.

Eyeliner next. Black, of course. Top and bottom. Whoa, her eyes looked huge! Still bruised but huge.

Lips? No gloss. Just lip liner. Riley found the pencil and managed to outline her lips in dark reddish-brown. A little crooked, maybe, but she didn't have time to fix it. She checked her teeth and wiped off the lip liner she'd accidentally gotten on one of her front teeth.

She heard a car pull up outside. Riley rushed to the window and peered out. It was the *Total Makeover* van.

Riley took one last look in the mirror, reminded herself to smile, and hurried downstairs.

A short time later Riley was dancing with Charlie at Xtreme. Streaming neon lights decorated the black walls, a live band blasted from a tiny stage, and there was free opening-night soda at the bar.

"So, kids, are you having a good time?" Dash called out from the edge of the dance floor.

"Oh, sure! Awesome!" Riley cried, a little breathless.

"Awesome?" Charlie asked skeptically.

"Okay, maybe not awesome," Riley admitted with a laugh. "But definitely good."

"You're being seriously decent about this," Charlie said.

[Riley: That's more like the Charlie I know and love! Though it's kind of weird that he's in such a good mood. I mean, here he is at a punk club dressed in California Cool. But he's still not very talkative. He seems distracted. I wish I knew what he was thinking about!]

"I bet you're glad this is the last night of the makeover," Riley said, scratching her cheek. The club was packed, and under the thick makeup her face itched from the heat.

Charlie nodded. He was scanning the club as he danced, as if he was looking for someone. Suddenly he waved.

Riley glanced over and felt her heart drop into her hefty boots. Now she knew what—or who—he was thinking about. Sierra!

"Be right back," Charlie said as the music ended.

"What's up, Riley?" Dash asked as Charlie hurried across the room.

Scratching her face again, Riley forced herself to smile. "A friend of ours just got here."

"Looks more like Charlie's friend than yours," Miri shouted as the music kicked in again.

"No, she's my friend, too," Riley said. At least she *was*, she thought to herself, watching Charlie introduce Sierra to some other kids.

Dash chuckled. "Are you sure about that? I think you and Charlie should have a talk, don't you?"

[Riley: I know—Dash just wants to see another argument. I guess he thinks it's funny or good for the show. But it's not funny to me! I mean, what's Sierra doing at a punk club? Did Charlie actually invite her? Is that why he's in such a good mood—because he's been waiting for her?]

Miserably aware that the camera was watching, Riley rubbed her itching face, smiled, and wondered what she should do.

• • •

Chloe walked up the deck steps and slid open the door to the kitchen. A stroll on the beach was not the answer to her problem. The answer was action.

No one was in the kitchen except Pepper, who trotted over for a head rub. "Hey, Pep," Chloe murmured, scratching the dog behind the ears. "What's happening? Is Mom still on the phone?"

Chloe listened but didn't hear her mother's voice. Maybe things *were* under control.

"Oh, no!" Macy's voice suddenly cried out from the office. "Not you, too!"

Then again, maybe they're not, Chloe thought. As she started toward the office, Manuelo rushed in.

"Manuelo, hi!" Chloe said. "What's going on?"

"What *isn't* going on—*that* is the question!" Manuelo shook his head. "Your mother still has not found a caterer or a hall. And now—ay! At the last second two models call to say they're sick and cannot work tomorrow!" He held up the empty coffee mug. "Your mother wants more coffee, and she is already like the jumping beans."

"Make some decaf," Chloe instructed. "She'll never know the difference."

"Excellent idea, my little crumpet. Oh!" Manuelo paused with his hand on a cupboard door. "Riley was looking for you. Let me see . . . she was upstairs with the makeup."

The makeup! Chloe's eyes snapped to the kitchen clock. She'd promised Riley she'd be here at five-fifteen. And it was after six!

Telling Manuelo she'd be right back, Chloe rushed upstairs to her room.

Riley was gone, of course, her makeup scattered across the top of the dresser.

[Chloe: How could I forget? Instead of helping my sister out, I went strolling along the beach! I can't believe how out of touch I've been. I ignored Lennon. I let Tara and Quinn down. And it was my fault Amanda got that C. I've been so busy de-stressing that I just created more stress!]

Feeling super guilty, Chloe began capping the tubes of makeup. As she closed the lid on the pale foundation, she noticed something on the label. She turned it over and read the ingredients.

"Oh, no!" she gasped. She grabbed her cell phone off the desk, powered it up, and quickly punched in Riley's number. While it rang, she frantically checked the labels on the rest of the makeup.

"Hi, this is Riley Carlson," Riley's voice mail announced. "I can't answer right now, but if you leave a message, I'll call you back!"

"Riley!" Chloe cried into the phone. "When you get this message, go wash your face—quick! That makeup you used? You're *way* allergic to it!"

chapter
ten

What am I going to do? Riley wondered again, watching Charlie and Sierra laughing and talking with the other kids.

"Gee, Riley, why don't you go join Charlie?" Dash asked from his position next to the camera.

> [Riley: That does it! I am not going to go start an argument just to make Dash happy. I'm going to keep smiling. Not because of this stupid contest. It isn't important anymore. Only Charlie is. And if I stop smiling, I'm afraid I'll start crying!]

"I think I'll get something to drink," Riley replied as cheerfully as possible. "This place is an oven!"

With the camera at her back, Riley headed for the soda bar. A drink was a good idea. Her face was itching like crazy.

Out of the corner of her eye she saw Sierra and

Charlie waving to her. Riley waved back and kept going. Squirming through dancing couples, she worked her way up to the bar and took a quick peek over her shoulder. Charlie and Sierra were back in conversation with the other kids. And Dash and the camera guy were stuck in the crowd. Good. Riley turned back to the bar.

The guy behind it stared at her through rimless glasses. "Are you okay?" he asked.

Not really, Riley thought. But how would he know?

"Could I have some ice water, please?" she asked, scratching her cheek.

The guy just stared at her.

"Um . . . water?" Riley repeated.

"Yeah, I heard you," he said. "Listen, don't take this wrong, but I think you'd better check out your face. It's kind of, well, puffy."

Puffy? What did *that* mean? Riley clapped her hands to her cheeks. They felt, well, *puffy*!

Riley hurried away from the bar, dodged through the crowd to the girls' bathroom, and stared at herself in the mirror.

The guy wasn't kidding. Her face—cheeks, eyelids, lips—was puffed up like a beach ball. A bright red beach ball!

The makeup! Riley realized, splashing water on her face. I must be allergic to it! Why didn't I read the labels?

The cool water felt good, but she knew it would take

a long time for her face to deflate. What was she going to do until then? Go back out in front of the camera? No way. In front of Charlie? Ha. He'd take one look at her basketball-sized face and find one more reason to drop her for Sierra.

Go home, Riley told herself. Call a taxi, and get out of here!

Riley slipped her cell phone out of her skirt pocket. But the battery was dead. Crossing her fingers that Charlie or Sierra or the crew wouldn't spot her, she called a taxi from the public phone outside the bathroom.

I can't just disappear, she realized. People might worry. She borrowed a pen from the guy behind the bar, scribbled a note on a napkin, and asked the bartender to give it to Charlie. At last, keeping her head down, she snuck through the crowd and made her escape.

As the taxi pulled away from Xtreme, Riley leaned back against the seat and sighed miserably. The contest was over and she knew they'd lost it for sure.

And what about Charlie? she wondered. That's the really important thing. Have I lost *him* for sure, too?

Riley's face still itched. She rubbed it gently with her fingertips, then felt her eyelids. Still puffy. She wouldn't look normal until at least tomorrow night—if she was lucky.

Tomorrow *night*? Mom's fashion presentation was tomorrow *afternoon*!

And I promised Chloe I'd model in it! Riley thought with a groan. How can I possibly model a line called Classical Elegance when my face looks like a deep-dish pepperoni pizza?

"Spicy cheese straws," Chloe said, reading from a recipe. "Puff pastry, cheese, of course, and chili powder. Roll, cut, sprinkle, bake. How hard can that be?"

"For you?" Manuelo teased.

Chloe laughed. "I know, I'm not exactly chef material. But this sounds pretty easy."

"It is," Manuelo replied. "I will let you have the honor while I put together my second-to-none shrimp puffs."

Chloe laughed again, then checked the clock. She'd kept trying to reach Riley, but her sister hadn't called back yet. "I wonder if Riley's still at the club," she said anxiously.

"No. I'm here," Riley said from the kitchen door.

"Riley!" Chloe cried. "Oh, no! Your face!"

"What's the matter? Fat, red, splotchy faces are in, don't you know?" Riley tried to joke, but Chloe could tell her sister felt awful.

"Sit, Riley," Manuelo ordered, pulling out a chair. "I will find some of that allergy cream."

"You heard him," Chloe said as Manuelo hurried from the room. "Sit."

Riley flopped into the chair.

"Oh, Riley, this is all my fault!" Chloe said. "Once I saw the makeup, I kept trying to call you."

"Dead battery," Riley explained.

"I'm really, really sorry I wasn't there for you," Chloe told her. "No excuses. But it'll never happen again."

"It's okay. But, Chloe, I can't be there for you now either." Riley pointed to her face. "Unless Mom lets me wear a bag over my head, I can't model looking like this!"

"Oh, no problem—you can wear a bag."

"Huh?" Riley's puffy eyes got bigger.

"Kidding," Chloe said. "You don't have to model. I'm going to. So are Tara and Quinn. They're thrilled."

"Wait a sec. Why are Tara and Quinn modeling?" Riley asked.

"Oh, right, you don't know what's been going on." Chloe quickly explained about the two sick models, the double-booked hall, and the caterers kitchen fire. "So I enlisted Tara and Quinn. Then I called Lennon, and he and his parents found us another place. Mom's checking it out now. Cross your fingers that I don't burn the cheese straws!"

Now Riley's puffy eyes looked skeptical. "You're making the food?"

"Don't sound so surprised!" Chloe laughed. "Okay, okay, *Manuelo* is making *most* of the food. We were going over recipes when you came in. But don't worry—we're going to stop and watch the last episode of *Total Teen*

Makeover later, and then we'll vote. I'll get out the ice cream, and we'll all watch together, okay?"

Riley groaned. "I don't want to watch a makeover show for a long time. Especially this one!"

Hmm. That didn't sound good. "Riley, what else happened tonight?" Chloe asked. "I mean, besides your face?"

Riley sighed. "Charlie invited Sierra to the club." Her voice caught a little. "I thought he was in a good mood because the show was almost over, and then I found out it was because of her! So I left."

"Without talking to him?" Chloe asked. "Or Sierra? Riley! You *have* to talk to them!"

Riley shrugged. "All I want to do right now is go to bed."

"Good idea," Chloe said. Not for one second did she think Charlie and Sierra were a couple, but she wasn't going to argue with her already unhappy sister. Not yet, anyway.

Later Chloe, Manuelo, and Macy settled in front of the television to watch *Total Teen Makeover*.

"Welcome to our special late-night segment showing the final clips from our teen makeover!" Dash Gilford said cheerfully. "This is the night you at home will register your votes for the winning couple! We'll have special phone lines open at the end of the show. And now, let's watch!"

First they showed highlights from the week, including some of the good-natured banter between Riley and Charlie. Actually Chloe thought it was pretty entertaining, though Riley would probably be embarrassed by it. Then she watched nervously as the program ran clips of the couples on their final dates. What would happen when Riley disappeared from the club? And would her face look like a balloon?

The guy from the Dunes School took his girlfriend bowling, which was pretty fun to watch, since she turned out to be better than he was. The second guy tried to teach his girlfriend how to stand up on a surfboard, and the third guy opted for a fancy restaurant and formal clothes, much to the shock of his super-casual girlfriend.

Finally Riley and Charlie appeared on the screen. Chloe peered closely, watching them dance together. Riley's face looked slightly pink, but it hadn't puffed up yet, thank goodness.

"Her hair is incredible!" Macy laughed.

Manuelo nodded. "Shellac, as I said. But not permanent. I *hope*," he added.

"Be right back," Charlie said, waving toward someone offscreen.

The camera focused in on Riley's face. "What's up, Riley?" Dash Gilford asked.

"A friend of ours just got here." Riley gave a forced smile and scratched her face again.

The segment ended there, and Chloe sighed with relief. It ended before Riley's face totally inflated.

Dash Gilford came back on. "And that's it, folks! You've seen all the clips, and now it's your turn to have your say. On the screen are four different numbers, one for each couple. We're ready to register your calls, so start dialing now!"

"Quick, Manuelo, call in the vote!" Chloe said excitedly.

Manuelo punched in the number for Riley and Charlie. "Done!" he said. "And now . . . back to shrimp puffs!"

Chloe jumped off the couch. She had a zillion things to do before bedtime. And she didn't feel stressed at all about being busy. She felt totally great!

chapter
eleven

Lying in bed early Saturday morning, Riley smelled muffins baking. Her stomach rumbled. No wonder, she thought. She hadn't eaten anything since late yesterday afternoon.

Her stomach rumbled again. Riley got up, padded into the bathroom, and forced herself to look in the mirror.

She'd showered last night, so her hair was back to normal. Her face didn't look like a red, overinflated balloon anymore either. Just a pink, *partly* inflated balloon.

Oh, well. Nobody was going to see her today anyway. She brushed her teeth, pulled on some terry shorts and a blue, stretched-out tee, and followed the muffin smell downstairs.

The doorbell rang as she headed for the kitchen. She changed direction and opened it. Her mouth dropped open.

"Riley!" Charlie said. "Can I come in?"

"Sure." She was so surprised to see him that she couldn't think of anything else to say.

[Riley: Great. Could I look any worse? Well, if he came to break up with me, I guess it doesn't matter!]

"What happened to you last night?" Charlie asked as he followed Riley into the living room. "I looked all over for you. Finally the bartender gave me a note on a napkin with water rings all over it."

"You mean you couldn't read it?" Riley asked.

"I finally figured it out. *Gotta go. Have fun. Later,*" Charlie repeated Riley's scribbled message. "What was *that* about? I kept calling and leaving messages. Why didn't you call back?"

"My cell phone was dead." Riley paused. "I was going to call you today." Maybe. If I was brave enough.

"But why'd you leave?" Charlie persisted.

"Look at my face." Riley pulled her hair back and tucked it behind her ears so he'd have a full view of her pizza face. "See?"

Charlie checked her out. "It looks kind of . . ."

"Pink. And puffy," Riley finished for him. Then she explained about her allergic reaction to the makeup. "But you should have seen it last night! It was like a red balloon. I didn't want anybody to see me like that. Especially you."

"Me?" Charlie's brown eyes were confused. "I don't care what you look like."

[Riley: Oh, great.]

"I love you for who you are," Charlie said.

[Riley: Hang on. Did he just say he loves me? Now I'm confused. What about Sierra?]

"What about Sierra?" she blurted.

[Riley: Well, that was smooth.]

"What?" Charlie looked even more confused. "What about Sierra?"

"Well, you were mad at me because of the makeover contest," Riley explained. "And then I saw you having all these heavy conversations with her. And then you invited her to the club last night, and you looked really happy to see her."

"I was, but . . ." Charlie stopped and put his hands on Riley's shoulders. "Listen."

"Okay." Riley took a deep breath, preparing for whatever was coming.

"One," Charlie said. "Okay, at first I was mad at you about the makeover. Then I was mad at myself. But I took it all out on you. And I'm sorry. Two," he went on. "I had exactly two so-called *heavy* conversations with Sierra. You want to know what they were about?"

Riley nodded.

"I really hated wearing those new clothes. I thought she'd get it because she hates how she has to dress for her parents," Charlie explained. "Well, she did get it. We talked about how hard it is when you can't express your own style."

Riley nodded. She hadn't realized that Charlie would feel as if she was cramping his style. She thought he understood that it was just for the show.

Charlie smiled. "The second time you saw us talking, I started to riff on the whole makeover thing, and she told me to get over myself and stop being such a brat."

Riley smiled. That sounded like Sierra!

"Three. I invited her to the club to meet my friend, Casey," Charlie said. "I was thinking they might hit it off. Besides, I thought she'd get a kick out of seeing the punk Riley. Four." He paused.

"Four?" Riley asked.

Charlie pulled her close and kissed her.

Riley put her arms around his neck and kissed him back. She had never felt so totally relieved in her life!

"I'm sorry about the contest," she said, pulling away a little. "Especially about the job at K-SUN. I know you really wanted it." She gazed up at him and smiled. "You sure you don't want me to organize at least a call-in campaign?"

"You don't have to," Charlie said with a big grin. "The manager called me at home half an hour ago. He saw me on the wrap-up show on TV, and . . . I got the job!"

"You're kidding!" Riley threw her arms around him again. "That is so cool! I'm so happy for you!"

Charlie laughed. "He said it was clear from the show that my heart belonged to punk. He could tell I had just the right quality for K-SUN."

"You mean grouchy?" Riley joked.

"Okay, I had that coming," Charlie admitted, laughing again. "I'm sorry, too. About the way I acted. I know you wanted to win the contest."

"It doesn't matter," Riley told him. And she meant it. She wasn't worried about the contest anymore. She and Charlie were back together again. Even better—they were never really apart!

"Riley!" Chloe called from the kitchen. "Telephone. It's Jenna!"

Riley and Charlie went into the kitchen, where they found Chloe rolling out puff pastry, Manuelo dicing shrimp, Macy going over a list, and Larry nibbling on millet. A basket of mini corn muffins sat on the counter. Riley tossed one to Charlie, grabbed one for herself, and picked up the phone. "Hello?"

"Riley!" Jenna squealed. "A bunch of us watched the show last night, and you Charlie were fantastic! You have *got* to win!"

"Thanks, Jenna," Riley said. "I don't know about winning, though. We sort of . . . argued, you know."

"I know—that was the best part!" Jenna cried. "It was just like you do on *The Morning Rant*, except we got to *see* you! Anyway, we all voted for you. I've got my fingers crossed!"

Riley hung up. "Jenna thinks we'll win because we argued," she reported. "Weird."

"But it *was* kind of natural," Chloe teased, sprinkling chili powder on the pastry.

"Natural's the best way to go," Larry agreed. "Except for this stuff." He wadded up the millet bag and popped a muffin into his mouth.

The phone rang again, and Riley picked it up. "Riley!" Sierra cried. "The show was totally great! You and Charlie are so perfect together! But what happened? Why did you disappear last night?"

Feeling guilty for ever suspecting her best friend, Riley explained about the makeup, but not about her silly suspicions. What could she say? She'd been seriously deluded!

The phone kept ringing. All Riley's friends called to say they'd voted for her and Charlie.

"Everybody loved the arguing," Riley reported, hanging up for tenth time.

"Yes, they loved the drama of it," Manuelo declared, chopping parsley. "People love the drama!"

"We were definitely a hit at West Malibu," Riley said. "I almost wish I'd watched the show."

"It was wonderful, sweetie," Macy said, stuffing her list into her bag.

"Even last night?" Riley asked. "What about my face?"

"They ended your segment before it blew up," Chloe assured her.

"Your face blew up?" Larry asked. "It looks intact to me."

Riley laughed as the phone rang again. "Hello?" she said, wondering which friend this would be.

"Riley Carlson?" a cheerful voice boomed.

"Yes?"

"This is Dash Gilford!" the television host announced.

"Dash . . . Mr. Gilford?" Riley asked.

Everyone in the kitchen came to a standstill, eyes on Riley.

"That's right!" Dash said. "I'm calling because the votes are in and counted. You and Charlie came in second place."

"Second," Riley repeated.

Everyone's shoulders slumped a little.

"The couple from the Dunes School won, but it was very, very close!" Dash said. "And the calls we got about you and Charlie were so enthusiastic, and all of us on the show liked you so much that we made an unusual decision."

"Decision?" Riley asked, shrugging at the questioning looks everyone was giving her.

"Yes! The winners chose the night on the town for their prize," Dash told her. "So we decided to award you and Charlie a second-place prize . . . the L.A. shopping spree!"

"Really?" Riley's voice rose to an excited squeak. She locked eyes with Charlie and gave him a thumbs-up. "I mean, thank you! Thank you so much!"

"It was our pleasure!" Dash boomed. "Have fun shopping in L.A!"

Thanking him again, Riley hung up. "We got the shopping trip!" she cried, racing across the room to hug Charlie. "The winners picked the night on the town, so the show gave us the shopping trip as the prize for second place! L.A. Music Factory, here we come!"

[Riley: Everyone went nuts! Charlie picked me up and twirled me around the kitchen. Chloe jumped up and down, accidentally spilling chili powder everywhere. Larry juggled mini-muffins and dropped them on the floor. Mom and Manuelo cheered. It would have made great television!]

"Whoa, we'd better get back to work!" Chloe said as everyone settled down. "We made kind of a mess."

As they cleaned up, Chloe called out her to-do list.

"Let's see . . . we've got the last of the shrimp puffs and cheese straws ready for the oven," she declared.

"Check," Manuelo said.

"And, Mom, you're going over to the hall now, right?" Chloe asked.

"Check." Macy pulled a huge fruit platter from the refrigerator and handed it to Larry. "Larry's coming to help me make sure there are enough chairs."

"Check," Larry said, carefully balancing the platter over his head as he went to the door.

"And I will load some extra chairs in the car, just in case," Manuelo said, following Larry out the door.

"Listen, I have to go, too," Charlie said to Riley. "I'll call you later, okay?" He gave her a kiss, said good-bye to Chloe, and left.

"It looks like you and Charlie are back together," Chloe said with a grin.

"We were never apart," Riley admitted.

"I knew it!" Chloe declared, putting two trays into the oven. "Don't worry. I won't say I *told you so.*"

"You just did." Riley laughed. "Speaking of being back—what about you? You're acting like the old Chloe."

Chloe shook her head. "I'm acting like the *real* Chloe, you mean. Yoga and meditation are great, but, honestly? I went way too far with all that. I mean, I actually went for a walk when Mom's presentation was falling apart. Then I forgot to help you with your make-up and look what a disaster *that* was!"

"Yeah, but don't feel bad about it anymore," Riley told her. "My face is okay. Well, it will be in a few hours. Plus it gave me a really good excuse to leave Xtreme extremely early!" Riley smiled wickedly. "And for that I seriously owe you!"

"Okay, I'll stop feeling guilty." Chloe laughed.

"Anyway, I finally figured out that so much de-stressing stressed me out! I missed spending time with Lennon and my friends and you. And I missed being busy and organizing things. Which reminds me, you're coming to Mom's presentation, aren't you?"

Riley giggled. "My puffy face and I wouldn't miss it."

"You know what is truly relaxing?" Chloe said. "Being yourself."

"No kidding," Riley agreed. "Look at all the stress I caused by trying to transform Charlie. Not to mention what happened when he turned me punk."

"You mean, turned you *pink*," Chloe teased, waving at Riley's face with a spatula. "So 'be yourself' should go right at the top of my to-do list."

Riley grinned. "Check!"

Mary-Kate and Ashley Sweet 16

Book 18: Suddenly Sisters

"I can't believe we're still talking about this," I said over my shoulder to my sister Ashley. "I've apologized about a million times."

We were standing in line at the cafeteria at school, waiting to pay for our lunches. For the fifth time that day, she had brought up the dress that I had borrowed for my date the weekend before. Well, borrowed and then ruined by spilling ketchup all over it.

"I just wish you had been more careful," Ashley replied, digging through her bag for her wallet. "I mean, that was my favorite dress."

She paid for our food and I led the way

through the cafeteria toward our usual table. Melanie Han and Brittany Bowen were already sitting there.

"Okay, say I *had* told you where we were going," I said, raising my shoulders slightly as I gripped my tray with both hands. "Would you have really said 'no'?"

Ashley paused and looked at me. I knew I had her. Neither one of us ever said 'no' when the other one wanted to borrow something.

"Okay, no. I wouldn't have said 'no,'" Ashley said finally, rolling her eyes. She flipped her long blond hair over her shoulder as she sat down. "But you still should have been more careful.

"All right, all right," I said, dropping into the chair next to Melanie. "I swear it will never happen again."

"Thank you," Ashley replied with a smile. "See, that's all you needed to say. And I promise I'll never take any of your stuff without thinking about where I'm going first."

"Deal," I said.

"I can't believe it," Melanie said with a gleam in her dark eyes. She put her book away and turned her attention to us. "You guys are *still* talking about the dress?"

"Not anymore, hopefully," I told her.

"Sheesh! At least it's only one dress, Ash,"

Brittany said. "I can't even tell you how many of my outfits have hit the Dumpster since my brother Lucas was born."

"What do you mean?" Ashley asked.

"The kid's like a walking disaster," Brittany said. "I mean, when he's not spitting up on you, he's throwing his food or knocking stuff over. And don't even get me started on the diapers."

"Oh! But he's so cute!" I said, thinking of baby Lucas's pudgy little cheeks and his dimpled arms and legs.

"Oh please," Brittany said. "I love the little guy, but my life has been insane since he came along."

"Well, when there's a baby around, you have to expect that kind of thing," Ashley said with a shrug. "Mary-Kate ruining my stuff is more *un*expected."

"All right! That's it! I'm never touching your stuff again!" I said with a laugh. "It's been decided!"

"Please! You guys, at least you *have* someone to borrow stuff from. You should appreciate it," Melanie said. "It stinks being an only child."

Ashley and I exchanged a look. Melanie's father was a fashion designer—that was where she got her eye for clothes. She hardly ever wore the same outfit twice.

"Why would you need to borrow stuff?" I asked. "Your dad brings home an entire new wardrobe for you every season."

"Yeah, Mel. You have the life," Ashley added.

"And I don't care what you say, Brittany," I put in. "I would love to have a little baby brother."

As I dug into my lunch, I saw Brittany and Melanie exchanging a mischievous look.

"What?" Ashley asked them.

"I was just thinking," Brittany said, folding her arms on the table. "If you guys think our lives are so great, why don't you come stay with us for a little while and see for yourselves?"

"Yeah. Ashley can stay with me and see if I really have 'the life,'" Melanie said. "And Mary-Kate can go stay with Brittany and the adorable baby."

"For how long?" Ashley asked, her eyes lighting up. Clearly she liked the idea.

"I don't know," Brittany said. "A week?"

I looked at Ashley across the table and we both smiled slowly. This could be very interesting.

"Sounds like fun," I said finally.

"Yeah," Ashley added with a nod. "We're in."

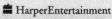

"So Little Time"
Apple iBook® Sweepstakes
OFFICIAL RULES:

1. NO PURCHASE OR PAYMENT NECESSARY TO ENTER OR WIN.

2. How to Enter. To enter, complete the official entry form or hand print your name, address, age, and phone number along with the words "*So Little Time*" Win an Apple iBook® Sweepstakes" on a 3" x 5" card and mail to: "*So Little Time* Win an Apple iBook® Sweepstakes", c/o HarperEntertainment, Attn: Children's Marketing Department, 10 East 53rd Street, New York, NY 10022. Entries must be received no later than May 28, 2005. Enter as often as you wish, but each entry must be mailed separately. One entry per envelope. Partially completed, illegible, or mechanically reproduced entries will not be accepted. Sponsor is not responsible for lost, late, mutilated, illegible, stolen, postage due, incomplete, or misdirected entries. All entries become the property of Dualstar Entertainment Group, LLC and will not be returned.

3. Eligibility. Sweepstakes open to all legal residents of the United States (excluding Colorado and Rhode Island), who are between the ages of five and fifteen on May 28, 2005 excluding employees and immediate family members of HarperCollins Publishers, Inc., ("HarperCollins"), Parachute Properties and Parachute Press, Inc., and their respective subsidiaries and affiliates, officers, directors, shareholders, employees, agents, attorneys, and other representatives and their immediate families (individually and collectively, "Parachute"), Dualstar Entertainment Group, LLC, and its subsidiaries and affiliates, officers, directors, shareholders, employees, agents, attorneys, and other representatives and their immediate families (individually and collectively, "Dualstar"), and their respective parent companies, affiliates, subsidiaries, advertising, promotion and fulfillment agencies, and the persons with whom each of the above are domiciled. All applicable federal, state and local laws and regulations apply. Offer void where prohibited or restricted by law.

4. Odds of Winning. Odds of winning depend on the total number of entries received. Approximately 300,000 sweepstakes announcements published. Prize will be awarded. Winner will be randomly drawn on or about June 15, 2005, by HarperCollins, whose decision is final. Potential winner will be notified by mail and will be required to sign and return an affidavit of eligibility and release of liability within 14 days of notification. Prize won by a minor will be awarded to parent or legal guardian who must sign and return all required legal documents. By acceptance of the prize, winner consents to the use of their name, photograph, likeness, and biographical information by HarperCollins, Parachute, Dualstar, and for publicity purposes without further compensation except where prohibited.

5. Grand Prize. One Grand Prize Winner will win an Apple iBook® computer. Approximate retail value of prize totals $1000.00.

6. Prize Limitations. Prize will be awarded. Prize is non-transferable and cannot be sold or redeemed for cash. No cash substitute is available. Any federal, state, or local taxes are the responsibility of the winner. Sponsor may substitute prize of equal or greater value, if necessary, due to availability.

7. Additional terms: By participating, entrants agree a) to the official rules and decisions of the judges, which will be final in all respects; and to waive any claim to ambiguity of the official rules and b) to release, discharge, and hold harmless HarperCollins, Parachute, Dualstar, and their respective parent companies, affiliates, subsidiaries, employees and representatives and advertising, promotion and fulfillment agencies from and against any and all liability or damages associated with acceptance, use, or misuse of any prize received or participation in any Sweepstakes-related activity or participation in this Sweepstakes.

8. Dispute Resolution. Any dispute arising from this Sweepstakes will be determined according to the laws of the State of New York, without reference to its conflict of law principles, and the entrants consent to the personal jurisdiction of the State and Federal courts located in New York County and agree that such courts have exclusive jurisdiction over all such disputes.

9. Winner Information. To obtain the name of the winner, please send your request and a self-addressed stamped envelope (residents of Vermont may omit return postage) to "*So Little Time*" Apple iBook® Sweepstakes Winner, c/o HarperEntertainment, 10 East 53rd Street, New York, NY 10022 after July 15, 2005, but no later than January 15, 2006.

10. Sweepstakes Sponsor: HarperCollins Publishers, Inc. Apple© Corporation is not affiliated, connected or associated with this Sweepstakes in any manner and bears no responsibility for the administration of this Sweepstakes

BOOK SERIES

Based on the hit television series

Mary-Kate and Ashley are off to White Oak Academy, an all-girl boarding school in New Hampshire! With new roommates, fun classes, and a boys' school just down the road, there's excitement around every corner!

Coming soon wherever books are sold!

Don't miss the other books in the TWO of a kind™ book series!

- ❑ It's a Twin Thing
- ❑ How to Flunk Your First Date
- ❑ The Sleepover Secret
- ❑ One Twin Too Many
- ❑ To Snoop or Not to Snoop?
- ❑ My Sister the Supermodel
- ❑ Two's a Crowd
- ❑ Let's Party!
- ❑ Calling All Boys
- ❑ Winner Take All
- ❑ P.S. Wish You Were Here
- ❑ The Cool Club
- ❑ War of the Wardrobes

- ❑ Bye-Bye Boyfriend
- ❑ It's Snow Problem
- ❑ Likes Me, Likes Me Not
- ❑ Shore Thing
- ❑ Two for the Road
- ❑ Surprise, Surprise!
- ❑ Sealed with a Kiss
- ❑ Now You See Him, Now You Don't
- ❑ April Fools' Rules!
- ❑ Island Girls
- ❑ Surf, Sand, and Secrets
- ❑ Closer Than Ever
- ❑ The Perfect Gift

- ❑ The Facts About Flirting
- ❑ The Dream Date Debate
- ❑ Love-Set-Match
- ❑ Making a Splash!
- ❑ Dare to Scare
- ❑ Santa Girls
- ❑ Heart to Heart
- ❑ Prom Princess
- ❑ Camp Rock 'n' Roll
- ❑ Twist and Shout
- ❑ Hocus-pocus
- ❑ Holiday Magic